THE EARTHQUAKE

Tahir Wattar

THE EARTHQUAKE

Translated from the Arabic and Introduction by
William Granara

Preface by
Gaber Asfour

Saqi Books

British Library Cataloguing-in-Publication Data
A catalogue record for this book is available from the
British Library

ISBN 0 86356 339 2 (pb)
ISBN 0 86356 944 7 (hb)

In-house editor: Jana Gough

Saqi Books
26 Westbourne Grove
London W2 5RH

Contents

To all the struggling workers, and to all those who have participated and continue to participate in the agricultural revolution in Algeria, who have a hand in laying sound foundations for a progressive democratic society.

T. W.

Author's Preface

I will not introduce myself as much as I will my work, a product of various cultural factors. I am merely one among one hundred million Arabs. There is no special value to my existence as a man struggling between two different mentalities; the first, medieval, general and abstract; the second, twenty-first century, scientific and technological.

As I've stated, my work is the product of a cultural dynamic within a certain area of the Arab world which has been, to some degree or another, exposed to the winds of an era which at times carried the seeds of life and, at other times, took those seeds away and replaced them with the seeds of death. I shall not expound.

The Earthquake is a novel from Algeria. The Arab reader may know much about Algeria during the time of colonial rule and its struggle for liberation. Algeria is a geography in every sense of the word. But does the reader know anything about Algeria after it won its independence?

In the aftermath of a century and a half of colonial rule, Algeria had to start from scratch. The policeman is new, as is the civil servant, the governor and the merchant. In fact both life and death are new. They are all part of a new entity which grew out of another entity, and then embarked upon establishing new structures and components of its identity.

In the end I may very well convince the educated Arab of the East that there does exist in Algeria a literature in the Arabic language. If his or her knowledge is restricted to Kateb Yacine and Malek Haddad, then this means that this knowledge is not very profound. Writers such as those are like hard currency, easily accessible throughout the world. Or it may mean that this restricted knowledge does an injustice to colleagues who try to contribute to enriching Arabic literature, or even to an entire people who struggle to reclaim one of the basic fundamentals of its identity, an identity that was and still is a target of colonial and imperial aggression. But above all, it does an injustice to the educated Arab, as an intellectual, by not bothering to reach out and look beyond the names of those who came into view by way of translation.

I would like to conclude by saying that socialist literature and the socialist hero in Algeria were given birth, as was cleverly pointed out by the late Jean Senac,[1] only in literature written in Arabic. As one who writes in Arabic, I take great pride and joy in that!

---

1. Jean Senac (1926–73), Algerian-born Francophone poet [*translator's note*].

Preface to the English Translation

The epic of change has been a dominant theme of the Arabic novel since its inception. Political, economic, social and cultural changes have taken place along with the growth of the modern city, still striving to overcome all obstacles hindering its growth until the present day. The epic of change evolves around the conflict between ancient and modern. The conflict arises with the realization that modernism and modernity are compatible: for the process of modernization to materialize, modernity has to be inscribed in the social consciousness. This becomes the intelligentsia's main preoccupation.

In the epic, the configuration of the ancient/modern binary is represented by the conventional forces striving to preserve a status quo that would maintain their economic, political, social and cultural interests. Change becomes a sign of forthcoming evil, or of a devastating earthquake destabilizing existence. Class consciousness informs the status of these conventional forces. It also implements a reductive vision of the cultural heritage, narrowing its confines to that which maintains their limited vision. The result is the construction of difference, a negation of diversity to sustain a patriarchal order. The disseminators of such beliefs reject modernity as heresy, making it as the initial step to final damnation.

The dialectical relationship between ancient and modern is represented in the Arabic novel through an insurgent consciousness. It focuses on the dilemma facing the elements of change on both the existential and political levels. Such elements interact with the modernizing process and react against conventional forces, blocking such a process. These conventional forces have never been highlighted in the narrative structure. In the early years of the century, there was no attempt to intuit the conceptual framework by which such conventional types abide, to perceive their strict conservative confines that resist change and try to deter it.

The few Arabic novels that have treated conventional types appear at a later stage. Earlier novels have mostly concentrated on revolutionary protagonists, seeking a rupture with the past in order to reconstruct a new order. Muhammad Hussein Heikal's (1888–1956) *Zaynab* (1914) is the first narrative attempt revealing a modernist consciousness. It traces the relationship of the rising intelligentsia with the conservative society. The purpose of the novel is to reconstruct the social order of a society dominated by conventionality. A series of fictional rebels later trailed in the Arabic novel: Kamal Abdelgawwad in Naguib Mahfouz's *Trilogy* (1956–57) is such an example, followed by other novelists of the succeeding generations.

Although these novelists have captured the continuous appearance of innovators at different stages of modernization, focusing on the problematic emerging from conflicting social needs, few have examined the rigid conceptual framework of conventional opponents to modernization, thus failing to shed light on the inherent motives driving them to shun diversity and innovation. There are even fewer attempts to analyse strategies of violent response that can become an act of virtual aggression against any challenge undertaken for progress.

Tahir Wattar (b. 1936) is one of the few novelists who have attempted to make up for the lack of conventional types in the Arabic novel. *The Earthquake* (first published in Beirut in 1974) presents a conventional figure who is an opponent of modernity. The narrator acts at times as subject, allowing the reader to listen to the inner voice, which is a strategy used in the stream of consciousness technique. Nevertheless, we still have a 'typological' study, to use Georg Lukács' term, where the typical refers to the universal, and the 'type' becomes a representative of what is yet to come.

This provides the novel with an additional function within its historical context. The changes affecting the dialectical relationship between tradition and innovation are connected to the changing relation between the typical and the general, the typical being the nucleus generating the general. Abdelmajid Boularwah – the protagonist characterized by typicality – becomes a general phenomenon in the Arab region. Echoes of Boularwah as conventional type recur in the Arab world, even though their opposition to modernization may be directed to different ends. Their targets differ simply because they have presently achieved more gains. They now succeed where Boularwah has failed due to the aggravating social conditions that have eventually empowered the oppressive forces. Allusions to such forces are made in Wattar's novel, and at times their presence is directly perceived.

Two decades after its first publication, the novel seems to be a forewarning of what is actually taking place at present. It features the dilemma in the Arab world on two levels: private and public. On one level, we follow up the protagonist, Shaykh Abdelmajid Boularwah's return to a changed Constantine, one that seems to have been struck by an earthquake. He is one of al-Zaytouna's fanatic graduates who later becomes the principal of a high school. He comes back to divide his property among his heirs, at least on paper, to avoid confiscation by the government. On another level, the change in the public sphere is brought about by a new state establishment that claims socialism and agricultural reform, while its newly constructed social order teems with contradictions.

Shaykh Boularwah's journey in place is a configuration of a spiritual journey. His movement throughout the transformed city ignites parallel shifts of consciousness at significant moments, evoking significant figures that have had a lasting impact. The alternating movement between past and present previews a devastating future. The aftermath becomes fully perceptible with Boularwah's end, bearing a multiple signification. However, the fact that he does not actually die, but is merely taken to hospital, raises the possibility of a future return. Indeed, his second return is marked by the resurgence of the political activists operating in Algeria today, who justify their terrorism with religious interpretations.

No wonder that the Algerian intelligentsia today are targeted by the terrorists, with the additional sacrifice of the very young and old. Most terrorists are high school graduates who were ideologically trained by principals similar to Shaykh Boularwah. They have multiplied in number, as have university graduates who were subjected to the same training. These graduates are the instigators of Algeria's present violence.

There is also in the novel a significant allusion to Naguib Mahfouz. Boularwah compares the Sidi M'sid district in Constantine to the Garabi' district in Mahfouz's *The Children of the Alley* (1959). Some have called this novel sacrilegious and accused Mahfouz of denying God's messengers their due respect. Boularwah accuses the Egyptians of cowardice for not putting Mahfouz to death. Ironically, Boularwah's wish was partially fulfilled two decades later (1994), when a young man attempted to assassinate Mahfouz six years after he had received the Nobel Prize for Literature. It seems that the young man was responding to Boularwah's *fatwa*. Mahfouz might have met the same fate as Abdelqadir Alloula, the Algerian dramatist assassinated by a Boularwah disciple who was trained in a similar high school administered by a Boularwah type. Such training fostered total rejection of all those branded as dissenters, particularly communists.

According to the shaykh, communists, liberals and existentialists are all infidels, followers of an alien West whose impact should be totally obliterated. Only then will the true faith be crowned with victory. Victory is attained by recruiting young people and making them blind followers who punish dissenters wherever they appear.

Although the implied narrator of *The Earthquake* alludes to the shaykh's fallen world, the narrative ironically forewarns of an imminent danger left by Boularwah and his disciples. Perhaps allusions to such a danger were inconceivable when the novel first appeared. However it lurks in the background as a premonition of a forthcoming disaster capable of aborting all dreams of emancipation. The narrative launches a strong criticism against the state, debunking the corrupt institutions that have contaminated its positive achievements.

Indubitably, such positive achievements arouse hopes for a better future. Boularwah's relatives better their condition by occupying higher social positions. His own impotence reveals the narrator's desire to eliminate his kindred, to ensure the removal of obstacles in the way of social democracy. Social democracy marks the destabilizing earthquake haunting Boularwah. His failure to adjust to the changing social conditions leads to a mental breakdown, a climactic moment in the narrative flow as Boularwah's withdrawal signifies a kind of moral punishment for his retrogressive stand.

In Algeria today, disaster is at hand. The nation lives in the aftermath of a devastating earthquake whose primal signs have erupted along the narrative flow, preceding the great downfall, extinguishing all hopes for democracy and justice. While Boularwah is defeated by the earthquake of progressive change, the present generation suffers the havoc created by terrorism. The earthquake bears a symbiotic nature revealing the common ground between binaries. The rebirth of Shaykh Boularwah in the existing conventional types creates another recessive cycle whose end is inconceivable in the near future.

Gaber Asfour
Professor of Arabic and Literary Criticism
Cairo University

Translator's
Acknowledgements

To all of the friends and colleagues who read the manuscript and made useful comments and suggestions I express my thanks: Roger Allen, Ayman El-Desouky, Seth Graebner, Susan Miller, Laila Parsons, Kristen Peterson-Ishaq, Barbara Romaine and Susan Slyomovics. I also wish to thank Gaber Asfour for encouraging me to undertake this project and for his thoughtful preface. Above all, I wish to thank Tahir Wattar for giving me the honour of translating such a masterpiece of modern Arabic fiction.

W. G.

Translator's Introduction

'I am a sick man . . . I am a spiteful man. I am an unattractive man.'
                                        Notes from Underground

This opening line of Fyodor Dostoevsky's 1864 novella in which the nameless hero introduces himself to the reader could just as accurately introduce Shaykh Abdelmajid Boularwah, the lone main character of Tahir Wattar's novel *The Earthquake* [*al-Zilzal*]. Both characters are subjects of psychological narratives which tell the story, in painful detail, of the inner turmoil of living on the edges of history and humanity.

The Earthquake is a novel about a character. The character, Shaykh Abdelmajid Boularwah, invades and pervades Wattar's novel from beginning to end. His every breath, move, thought and action give this work its form and substance. The grotesque physique, the wobbling, rotund body sweating profusely in the murderous Constantine sun, and the spiteful, cantankerous and conniving personality come together and mould a most interesting and complex literary figure. Readers of Western literature may find in it similarities with Rabelais' (d. 1553) Pantagruel, his literary construction through which he sought to satirize the religious, cultural and legal institutions of sixteenth-century France. One is more immediately reminded of Alfred Jarry's (d. 1907) Ubu Roi, the central character in a theatrical trilogy, whose grotesque body, repulsive manners and vulgar speech were created to assault the artistic and ethical sensibilities of bourgeois French society and whose opening night in 1896 sent shock waves throughout even the most libertine of Parisian theatrical circles.

In the same vein, Shaykh Abdelmajid Boularwah is a shocking character. In fact, he is more than a man in physical, mental and spiritual decline; pathetic like the nameless narrator of *Notes from Underground*, and spiralling out of existence like Jean-Baptiste Clamence, the narrator of Albert Camus' novel *La chute* [The Fall] (1956), Shaykh Abdelmajid Boularwah is truly evil, a character completely devoid of any saving grace.

Ironically, the reader of modern Arabic fiction may find Shaykh Abdelmajid Boularwah more difficult to place. He or she may see him as somewhat of a surprise, if not an anomaly. It is indeed rare to find in modern Arabic literature an unequivocally evil character as a central figure. Certainly, there are all kinds of villains and antagonists: swindlers, profligates, traitors and collaborators, killers, drug addicts, deserters and social outcasts. The difference is that these characters are cast in the margins of both the narrative and social discourse. They are constructed to serve as victims of society's ills, as symbols of religious, social and political aberrations. They are the constructs of a particular kind of didacticism that underlines the social and ethical dimensions of modern Arabic literature. In the end, one way or another, they reintegrate into society or they fade away into literary condemnation.

The modern Algerian novel makes its first appearance in the French language in the 1950s, at the time when Algerians were engaged in a struggle for national liberation from a century of French colonial rule that began with France's conquest of Algeria in 1830.[1] Their war for independence, which Algerians call 'The War of a Million Martyrs', began in 1954 and ended with independence in 1962. Naturally, this long, hard-fought struggle figures prominently in the shaping of this new novel. As Aida Bamia observes, 'This burning desire to reveal their existence and their true nature to the world characterized the

---

1.   Among the most important early Algerian novels written in French are Mouloud Feraoun's *Le fils du pauvre* (1950), Mohammed Dib's *L'incendie* (1954), Mouloud Mammeri's *Le sommeil du juste* (1955), Kateb Yacine's *Nedjma* (1956) and Assia Djebar's *La soif* (1957). One of Algeria's best-known novelists, Rashid Boudjedra (*La répudiation*, 1969), began writing his novels in Arabic in 1981.

beginning of a national Algerian literature.'[1] This new-born novel, written in the language of the colonist, and being the only language available to many of its writers, confronted the enemy in their own idiom and, at the same time, sought to articulate an Algerian national consciousness and identity.[2] Most important, this first-generation Algerian novel brought attention to the misery of both urban and rural poverty, as well as the social injustice suffered by the indigenous population at the hands of the colonial government and the communities of privileged European settlers.

The first Arabic-language novels in Algeria, by contrast, come almost a decade after independence. The events of the long and bitter struggle and the bitter memories of it provide both the context and the inspiration for these first Arabic novels.[3] The political, social and religious disputes that formulated the modern Algerian national discourse, and which were set aside in common cause in the struggle against French occupation, resurfaced in this new Arabic fiction in its various characters, plots, settings and points of view. In a very real sense, the Arabic Algerian novel is a post-colonial novel.

Tahir Wattar is a pioneer of the Arabic novel in Algeria. He was born in eastern Algeria in 1936, received a traditional (religious) education in Algeria and studied at the prestigious al-Zaytouna University in Tunisia where he lived during most of the war of independence. After his return to Algeria he wrote for literary journals before launching his own career as a writer. He has written plays and collections of short stories but is most widely known for his novels

---

1. Aida Bamia, 'The North African Novel: Achievements and Prospects', in *The Arabic Novel Since 1950, Mundus Arabicus*, Vol. 5 (Dar Mahjar, Cambridge, 1992), pp. 61–89.

2. I am not concerned here with novels written by European citizens of colonial Algeria, e.g. Albert Camus, nor, for that matter, with Francophone literature produced in Algeria in the decades preceding the rise of Algerian nationalism (*c.* 1930). See Bamia, 'The North African Novel', p. 63. However, some of these works do, in fact, express a particular Algerian (vs. French) sympathy. See Jonathan Gosnell, 'Assertions of "Algerianité": Intellectual Production of a Colonial Identity', *Romance Review*, VI, no. 1 (Autumn 1996), pp. 85–95.

3. For a discussion of the history and early development of the Arabic novel in Algeria, see Muhammad Masayif, *al-Riwaya al-'arabiyya al-jaza'iriyya al-haditha: bayna al-waqi'iyya wa al-iltizam* (al-Dar al-'arabiyya li-l-kitab, Algiers, 1983). Also see Bamia, 'The North African Novel'.

(see bibliography). Wattar's first novel *al-Laz* [The Ace], written between 1965 and 1972 and published in 1974, and its sequel, *al-Laz: al-'ishq wa al-mawt fi al-zaman al-harashi* [al-Laz: Love and Death in Terrible Times], published in 1982, are prime examples of this Algerian Arabic independence literature.[1]

His second novel, *The Earthquake*, was also published in 1974. If *al-Laz* is to be considered his 'classic' novel of the Algerian struggle for independence, then *The Earthquake* is Wattar's 'classic' post-colonial novel. In it there is much that draws upon both Western and Arabo-Islamic literary traditions and themes (which will be discussed in some detail below), a key factor that distinguishes the Arabic novel in Algeria from its French counterpart. Beyond the mere difference of language, the Arabic novel delves into a history, a religion, a mentality that most Algerians share with a huge number of Muslims and Arabs, past and present, in ways that the French novel of Algeria has failed – or chosen not – to do.

Reading Tahir Wattar's *The Earthquake* is a challenging enterprise. In no way could it serve as an easy 'entry' into modern Arabic – or even Algerian – literature. In addition to its 'cultural' complexity, there is the stark, consciously unaesthetic, black-and-white prose, the sudden and frequently shifting stream(s) of consciousness from the third-person narrative to first-person monologues, interspersed with dialogues that take place in both the present and the past, all the classic literary devices of the modern novel that challenge the reader to interpret its meanings. The embedding of stories within stories, evocative of the narrative technique of *A Thousand and One Nights*, has at times a dizzying effect. The bleak descriptions of strewn garbage, the stench of human filth, images of urban poverty and suffering, and recollections of heinous crimes against the innocent, force the reader to share in the experience of Wattar's disturbing visions of an imaginary universe, of a society going wrong.

The basic structure of the novel is the journey (*rihla*), a popular subgenre in Arabic literature in all its phases. Shaykh Abdelmajid

---

1. For a brief summary and analysis of these two works, see Muhammad Siddiq, 'The Contemporary Arabic Novel in Perspective', *World Literature Today*, 60, no. 2 (Spring 1986), pp. 206–11; also, Roger Allen, *The Arabic Novel* (Syracuse University Press, Syracuse, 1995), pp. 80–1.

Boularwah sets out from the capital, Algiers, and drives nine hours to Constantine (site of an actual earthquake in 1947) in search of relatives in whose names he intends to register his land in an attempt to prevent the government from nationalizing his property. Thus the plot follows faithfully the historical reality of agrarian reform which was one of the cornerstones of the post-independence restructuring of the 1970s. The novel begins with his arrival in Constantine, and all of its events take place, reminiscent of Joyce's *Ulysses* (1922), in one long, tortuous afternoon. His quest to deceive the government in its campaign to launch a programme of agrarian reform leads Boularwah through a labyrinth of back alleys and past memories. In the process he becomes the consummate rogue, the deceitful trickster whose chaotic adventures and reminiscences, both real and imaginary, derail this journey into the picaresque. As he traverses the city of Constantine, precariously perched high on a rock, and makes his way across its seven bridges, he battles the forces of a rapidly changing society while confronting the demons of his past. The sequence of his recollections constructs an autobiographical narrative whose subject, a defiantly proud scion of a family of ruthless, rural landowners, swindlers, traitors and collaborators with the colonial authorities, tells his story of modern Algeria from a consistently adversarial and surrealistically twisted point of view.

The young Abdelmajid Boularwah's journey to Tunisia to receive an 'Islamic' education and his return to Algeria as a man of religion and learning provide the sharp ironic tone of the novel. It is also in keeping with a traditional motif of 'the satire of religion endemic to the picturesque'.[1] His vocation as a traditionally educated headmaster of a high school associates him with the class of Muslim clerics, often the subjects of lampoons in modern Arabic literature. Throughout the Arab – and Muslim – world, much of twentieth-century culture and politics has centred around debates pitting tradition against modernity, East against West, religious against secular, and faith against science and technology. It was the cleric, clothed in medieval robe and turban, defender of the rich and exploiter of the poor,

---

1. Barbara A. Babcock, '"Liberty's a Whore": Inversions, Marginalia, and Picaresque Narrative', in *The Reversible World: Symbolic Inversion in Art and Society*, ed. Barbara A. Babcock (Cornell University Press, Ithaca, 1972), p. 103.

collaborator, government informant, anti-progressive, hypocrite and sinner, who stood for all that was wrong and all that was in need of change. Wattar's *The Earthquake* follows in this tradition.

As a 'man of the cloth', Shaykh Abdelmajid Boularwah may be read as the subject of the classic mock-heroic parody in whose composition the exemplarity of the ideal imam or shaykh – the Prophet Muhammad – is implied. Both the historical and literary (textual and popular) figure of the Prophet, and, by extension, the ideal imam, is just, caring, selfless, temperate in his bodily appetites, nurturing, inclusive, tender and affectionate with women, and generous and gentle to the poor and weak. Shaykh Abdelmajid Boularwah is none of the above. In fact, his persona is a composite of all of the opposite attributes. He is the anti-Muslim hero in Wattar's *anti-roman*.

The euphoria of victory in post-colonial, independent Algeria was short-lived. No sooner had the armistice been signed and a new republic declared than old rifts and rivalries resurfaced. Scores had to be settled, collaborators punished, and Algeria witnessed a massive exodus of many of its citizens, draining the country of much of its expertise. The economy suffered, there was mass dislocation, particularly from rural to urban centres, and the population exploded. It is in the context of these problems and the new government's socialist revolution, its ambitious agrarian reform, its large-scale industrialization, its goals of Algerianizing a new, massive state apparatus, and Arabizing culture and education, that the text of *The Earthquake* is best understood.[1] Wattar's vision of post-colonial Algeria is of a society in chaos, a 'world upside down', and to give literary expression to this vision he taps into the rich corpus of Islamic eschatological imagery and apocalyptic legends, and reworks their symbols of inversion to reinforce the ironic mode of the novel.

It is the Qur'an and, more often, the *hadith*, the corpus of sayings and actions of the Prophet Muhammad, that provide the bases for Islamic apocalyptic legends. The title of the novel is taken from the title of Chapter 99 of the Qur'an which foretells the Day of Judgement.

---

1. For a succinct and well-balanced account of modern Algerian history, see Charles-Robert Algeron, *Modern Algeria: A History from 1830 to the Present*, tr. & ed. Michael Brett (Hurst & Co., London, 1991).

The first two verses of Chapter 22 (The Pilgrimage), *Every suckling female will forget her suckling, and every pregnant female will discharge her burden, and you will see men drunk, yet it will not be in intoxication*, which offer a glimpse of the state of the world at the end of time, constitute a kind of mantra which Shaykh Boularwah chants in his wanderings throughout Constantine as he, in his self-appointed role as harbinger of doom, tries to prevent the new government and its supporters nationalizing his extensive property. Images of the apocalypse, fire and smoke, flooding, earthquakes and eschatological motifs, transformations in nature, the man on the beast that will roam the earth (the Antichrist), etc give both a concreteness to Boularwah's vision of the disorder of Constantine and a religious authority to his sanctimonious reactions to it.[1] Through them he rationalizes a world no longer under his control, slipping away from him as fast as is his own sanity. It is a world wedged between two realities, two pasts and two futures.

The ambivalence of Shaykh Abdelmajid Boularwah's *world upside down* allows for variations in reading this novel, particularly from our vantage point of hindsight. In Todorov's terminology,[2] the signification of the text allows us to get a glimpse of the Constantine (of Algeria) of the early 1970s and we may even correctly guess Tahir Wattar's political affiliations and aspirations. But it is its *symbolization*, the bite of his irony, the focus of his parody and the vividness of his images of inversion that 'permit those satisfied with the existing or traditional social order to see the theme as a mockery of the idea of changing that order around, and at the same time, those dissatisfied with that order to see the theme as mocking it in its present, perverted state'.[3] The recurrence of apocalyptic themes and

---

1. One frequently mentioned *hadith* is as follows: 'The hour of doom will not appear until you see ten signs: smoke; the Antichrist; the beast; the sun rising in the west; the appearance of Jesus, son of Mary; Gog and Magog; and three solar eclipses, one in the east, one in the west and one in the Arabian peninsula; and the last, a great fire coming from Aden that will smoke out the people from their hovels.' Quoted in Ibn Kathir, *'Alamat yawm al-Qiyama*, ed. 'Abd al-Latif 'Ashur (Dar Bouslama, Tunis, 1983), p. 58.

2. Tzvetan Todorov, *Genres in Discourse*, tr. Catherine Porter (Cambridge University Press, Cambridge, 1990), pp. 42–3.

3. David Kunzle, 'World Upside Down: The Iconography of a European Broadsheet Type', in Babcock (ed.), *The Reversible World*, p. 82.

imagery provides the novel with a rhythm and resonance that give a psychological coherence to the actions of the novel and, at the same time, help to transmit its political messages and define its aesthetic distances.

Algeria of the 1970s was a vast historical and geographic cross-roads. It lay between colonialism and independence, French and Arabic, Europe and the Arab world, Islam and socialism; it stood between a hard-fought struggle for self-determination and an uncertain future of battling ideologies, between hope and despair, sanity and insanity. Shaykh Boularwah's odyssey takes us from past to present, from stoic reality to surrealism, from one opposite, one extreme, to the other. Wattar's novel is an indictment, an auto-da-fé, against the old guard, the old institutions and the forces of recidivism. But do the powers of modernity, the new order, the new regime, fare much better?

Algeria of the 1990s has taken an unexpected turn, torn apart once again into two pasts, two futures, two visions in conflict. Its political and social situation resonates clearly an apocalyptic legend in which the Prophet Muhammad describes the signs of the end of the world:

> When the spoils of war [the state treasury] is not divided lawfully; when Islam is embraced for profit; when alms are given grudgingly; when men obey their wives but disobey their mothers; when people are kind to their friends but ignore their fathers; when voices are raised in the mosques; when the leader of the people hails from its lowest ranks; when a man is honoured out of fear of his evil deeds; when wine is consumed and silk is worn; when singing girls and musical instruments abound; when the young generations curse fathers and grandfathers; then they can expect a violent wind, a black sky, or a great shake-up of the earth.[1]

The excitement of Tahir Wattar's *The Earthquake* lies in his ability to expand the boundaries of these legends and rework them into a new Arabic literature and its political and social contexts and subtexts. Its brilliance lies in its timeless message against a sick, spiteful and

---

1. Cited in Ibn Kathir, *al-Fitan wa al-malahim fi akhir al-zaman*, ed. Yusuf 'Ali Badiwi (Dar Ibn Rushd, Beirut, 1993), p. 37. The translation is mine.

unattractive extremism, the seismic shocks of which Tahir Wattar so presciently felt long before they reappeared.

Bab al-Qantara
(The Bridge at Qantara Gate)

The sense of smell overwhelms all other senses in Constantine. You are assaulted by one odour or another with every step, every glance and every breath you take. It's usually an obnoxious odour that grates on your nerves and weighs heavily on your heart.

Shaykh Boularwah was thinking to himself as he opened his car door, after parking in a tight space which had taken him a long time to find. It was in the small square which stood across the Bridge at Qantara Gate. He took a long, deep breath and straightened his jacket. He looked at his watch carefully as he thought about what to do next.

A quarter to. A nine-hour drive from Algiers. What a journey in this heat! Constantine is like the Kaaba, it brings good luck when you enter it on Friday!

He locked the doors, turned around and headed up towards Ben M'hidi Street. He stared out for a moment onto the horizon, then turned back towards the car. He went over to inspect it once again to make sure that he had locked all the doors.

The train whistle blew. It annoyed him because it was louder and longer than necessary. Was it a last warning signal? No, just a brazen statement of the anguish its passengers feel whenever they come to Constantine.

He found himself staring at the bridge. For some strange reason he felt a modicum of composure despite the thick traffic and the crowds of men and women frantically passing by him.

He thought to himself:

All these people, all these cars moving about all at once. I nearly forgot what life is like in Constantine!

Before looking up and moving on, he thought how much nicer this bridge was than the others in Constantine, wide yet short enough to let people forget the awesome chasm that lies between it and the river below.

From that angle everything seemed to him as it always had, the greenness of the trees and all the different buildings he could easily identify. There was the high school, the hospital and the odd-shaped granary, built for the sole purpose of serving as some everlasting proof that the city was first and foremost an agricultural centre. Perhaps its builders meant to remind the citizens that there existed storage space for wheat and barley, and that if they ever found themselves under a prolonged state of siege they would not die of starvation. Ah, and then there was the winged statue of Joan of Arc, ready to take off God knows where and for how long. And of course there was the suspension bridge, Constantine's most sacred object.

Shaykh Abdelmajid Boularwah's heart fluttered when he noticed the suspension bridge. He took another look at the hospital, the granary and the high school, the villas and trees. Doesn't it look cleaner than it used to, he wondered, brighter, more colourful? Hasn't the dull, drab European colour faded? Also, doesn't it seem to tilt more as if it wanted to look out over the depths of the vast ravine? I have no idea whatever possessed the Rhumel Valley to open itself up to the heart of a city so preoccupied with itself.

Shaykh Abdelmajid Boularwah was heartened by the sound of the call to prayer and convinced himself to continue up the road inundated with the aromas of fragrant plants, roasting meats and vegetables, and exotic perfumes, and bustling with the comings and goings of cars and people in every direction.

There is no power or strength save in God! What makes people walk in such a way in this city? And here I am, finally, after I nearly had to abandon my car in the middle of the street. I was so afraid that they'd swarm over it like flies on the Day of Resurrection. What possesses these people to push and shove the way they do, coming and going, back and forth, alone or in crowds, and in such hot weather?

It is true, I've forgotten Constantine.

No. In fact, the city has been turned upside down. It was peaceful at the time of the French, very noticeably so. Life began at the crack of dawn, slowly, leisurely, and it burst into full bloom between ten o'clock and noon. Then it would suddenly quieten down until three o'clock only to resume its hustle and bustle between five and nine, when all the schools would let out their students, and the lights shone bright. You could inhale the fragrance of the perfume of the European and Jewish girls who filled the streets with rapture and joy like the virgins of paradise.

But everything has changed. Ibn Khaldoun was on the mark when he . . .

No, no! We struggled so that Algeria would be Arab and we will never regret it.

We opposed this view of Ibn Khaldoun at the beginning of independence and all throughout the following years until they started to veer away from the subject and announce some new idea or another, coming from God knows where. But they blew it all out of proportion. They've gone too far. They deceived us. At first they introduced socialism with simple slogans, but then they started to take it more literally until it became a word which had to mean something. And now suddenly . . .

No, no.

Freedom, independence, power and authority, that's all well and good. But operating on the body of the living to the point of desecration? Never!

We studied sacred scriptures and sat at the feet of our learned, pious teachers. We fought on the side of our reformist hero, Ibn Badis. May God shower him with His infinite mercy! We mastered the precepts of the four schools of Islamic law, but we never anticipated this abomination.

No! A thing belongs to its rightful owner. Private property is guaranteed to us in the holy Qur'an. People are content with their lot in life, satisfied with the blessings God has apportioned to them, except that they blindly rush to the Day of Judgement.

Someone came along and shoved Shaykh Boularwah with his shoulder and pushed him off the narrow sidewalk. At that moment a car came to a screeching halt as the driver slammed on his brakes and shouted at him in anger. A succession of screeching tires followed, along with the thumping of scraping fenders. People began to gather and children started to yell and scream. The shaykh looked around and, noticing a hole in the crowd, pushed his rotund body through it. He moved quickly and left the crowd. Without thinking he pulled his watch out of his pocket to check the time.

The time has come, he thought to himself.

He decided to quicken his pace and shorten the distance that separated him from the Grand Mosque. However, a strange but oddly familiar voice caught his attention and made him stop. The voice was calling out, shouting angrily:

'This city has become much too congested, my good sir! Five hundred thousand inhabitants instead of the one hundred and fifteen thousand that were here when we were colonized. Half a million, my good sir. The whole lot of them are overflowing from the top of this great big rock. They left their villages and deserts and invaded our city. They filled every inch of it until there wasn't any space left to breathe. They've sucked up all the air and left in its place the stench of their armpits.

'O, Sidi Rashid, man of miracles, come forward and pronounce your sentence. Shake this rock and rid it of these people, their impiety, corruption and debauchery. It's time for you to come, Sidi Rashid, it's time. You've been much too patient, O worker of miracles.'

He looked around to see whose voice was speaking and found that it was that of an old townsman wearing a tall red fez and standing at the doorway of the Café Najma. He was waving his hands in the air as though he were pleading. Shaykh Boularwah stole a quick glance first at the line of people waiting at the entrance to the elevator, then at the narrow bridge suspended by wire cables, and finally at the vast ravine which divided the two banks of the river and stood as a barrier between one part of the city and the others. He glanced at the smooth rock sloping along the two sides of the ravine. Between the bend and its curves lay trees and grottoes. There were black and white pigeons hovering above, flapping in the wind like pieces of fluffy wool. Shaykh Boularwah felt a strange sensation coming over him. He sensed that a certain colour, very dark, was infiltrating his heart. He tried to block out the sensation, or the colour, but then started to talk out loud as though he had suddenly forgotten what was going on.

He says that they left the villages and deserts and invaded the city. What does he expect them to do in the villages and deserts? Did they descend upon people's property and seize it from them? It's true that they're lazy and no longer satisfied with working the land. But they came to the city so that the government would give them jobs. The government has to build factories for them and put them to work. Or at least they should send them abroad, allow them to leave, something that has become more and more difficult of late. Instead of taking care of these people, the government decided to preoccupy itself with pious people to whom God has bequeathed His land.

God damn them . . .

These townspeople, they're all the same! They want to monopolize the city. They make no bones about keeping outsiders from getting any part of it.

At the entrance to the Grand Mosque Shaykh Abdelmajid Boularwah watched the faces of the beggars as they stood in a row against the wall. He noticed something peculiar about the city. The faces are all different in Constantine. Facial features vary from one person to another, as do people's physiques. At the time of the occupation, people looked either European or Arab, but not now. Today, you can tell the difference between the Shawi Berber from Ain Baida or Ain M'lila, from Banta, Khanshala or Shalghoum al-Id. You can tell who is from Fajj M'zala, Milia or Collo, or from Skikda, Zenah and Azzaba. Their facial features, like their odours, reveal their true identities in loud screams that echo throughout the city.

Forcefully, he pushed away the hand of a beggar woman who got in his way, then took off his shoes and headed towards the door of the mosque.

'Take your hand off me,' he mumbled in disgust. 'God help us! What a disaster! Where did they all come from? Why don't you all go back to your villages and deserts?'

'May a disaster fall on your head! You talk as though you're carrying us all on your shoulders like we're some kind of burden on you.'

The woman shouted back angrily in an accent that Shaykh Abdelmajid recognized as being from the Tunisian border, and he thought how brazen and insolent she was. He turned around suddenly and stared for a good while, then decided to forget what he was thinking of saying to her as well as to the rest of the crowd.

A rock is carrying us all, he thought, especially you and your kind. At every tide the water does its damage. God knows how many holes are inside this rock, and at any moment, in its own peculiar way, it could cry out what a burden we all are.

He noticed again the waving hands of the old townsman in the fez, who was still shouting:

'O Sidi Rashid, man of miracles . . . shake off these people, their impiety and corruption.'

He regained his composure long enough to continue making his way through the line towards the mosque. His shoes were in his hands, while a strange, dark, shadowy feeling was building up inside him, seizing him.

He straightened himself up and prepared to perform his prayers. He imagined the great reformer Shaykh Ibn Badis in the pulpit with his animated expression. It was nothing like the stone-faced image artists used to try to depict him in some idealized fashion, artists who thought that knowledge was better expressed by dumb-witted meditation and naive dignity than by dynamism and intellectual curiosity. It occurred to him that this image of Ibn Badis was very different from the one he himself harboured of the venerated shaykh throughout the years that followed his death, and indeed it was very strange, given all the events that occurred at that time. He was a stranger to all of us, he thought, despite the great enthusiasm we all had for him. He was like an overflowing river, every part of it flowing towards the source, while we . . .

Shaykh Boularwah abhorred the idea of completing such an admission, the truth of which was so plainly evident in the real-lifeness of this image of Ibn Badis. He was content to think out loud: Had he lived, he would have had a great effect on us. But religion is religion and nothing more. Religion is being loyal to our ancestors. Any reckless innovation leads us astray.

He resumed his prayers and stopped thinking about Ibn Badis. It was actually the movement of his right index finger that made him forget. It had automatically moved sideways with an unusual speed. Then it began to grow sluggish, slowly, gradually, until it finally stopped. Suddenly it started to move up and down, shaking back and forth until it stopped for a moment only to move in a strange circular motion.

God damn Satan, that perfidious tempter. He brought back this shaking movement to my finger which was the reason for my expelling that student from class. I wonder what happened to him.

The students used to call him the philosopher. I called him the heretic. I felt no sympathy whatsoever towards him in spite of his gentle manner. The more he tried to approach me and talk to me, the more I felt that I was standing before someone who could read what was inside me. I thought I was standing face to face with my enemy. Only the Lord up above knows secrets, but that evil heretic could look straight through people and peer into their souls.

He asked me during class one day:

'Sir, does God up in heaven, master of the universe, determiner of the fates of all planets, the heavens and the earth, find enough time to inspect the movement of every index finger during prayer? Does it offend Him if the movement is up and down instead of sideways? And does he concern himself with the worshipper whose finger or hand is cut off?'

I let him finish his question then I berated him:

'You're dismissed! I swear on the head of the Prophet Muhammad, the intercessor for all Muslims, that you are absolutely, positively expelled! Get out of here, son of Satan!'

He coughed, then picked up his briefcase and left the mosque proudly, with his head held high. Curse the Devil, and here I am making the same movement all over again. That incident happened twenty-three years ago, and now it's come back to my finger.

He leaned against the wall of the mosque to put on his shoes. Then he clutched his bulging stomach with both his arms, sweat pouring down his face as he tried to slip on his shoes. His large bulging eyes opened wider and his lips quivered as he recited a prayer. The muscles of his face relaxed, then grew limp.

'No, this coin fell from my pocket.'

'No, from mine.'

'O, God's loved ones!'

'May He save and protect you.'

'Think of God and of your parents.'

'I was first!'

'No, I was.'

The voices of the beggars droned in his ears while the stench of their dirty bodies assaulted his nose. There was also the aroma of a roasting sheep's head and the rancid smell of stale pastries, mixed with the scent of jasmine and discarded prickly pear rinds.

The sounds of Constantine are like its odours and facial features. They have their own distinctive personality. Why didn't I notice it during the days of colonial rule? No! The city has changed. It's swarming with people, a million and a half sitting on a rock! That's too much.

That feeling of a strange, dark shadow was once again creeping up inside him.

Instead of using the occasion of the Friday sermon to address issues of piety, the imam spoke about the Earthquake of Doom. He explained at length how the actual earthquake is described in the

Qur'an: 'Every suckling female will forget her suckling, and every pregnant female will discharge her burden, and you will see men drunk, yet it will not be in intoxication.'[1] There will be disorientation, confusion, restlessness and the feeling of a dark shadow invading men's souls. This is how Almighty God has described the condition at the end of time, and he has used the earthquake to illustrate how that final hour will come.

'God help you!' he said to a young girl, as he put his coins back into his pocket, having failed to find a five-franc coin, and only finding tens and twenties. He forced himself to keep on walking. He took each step nervously while his chest and buttocks wobbled along with the rest of his body. His head dangled from side to side while he kept his arms wrapped around his stomach.

I'll get a bite to eat, whatever I can find, he thought. I'll still have enough time if I can push ahead of these bastards. He stepped up his pace and moved swiftly as he crossed the narrow street. He jumped onto the sidewalk and stood at the entrance to a square that connected to many side streets and passageways, some ascending, some descending, some partly roofed, while others were totally exposed.

The main boulevard is as it always was. The prickly pear vendors are still at their stalls and the other vendors are in theirs selling the same goods they always did. And then there are the same old songs. Issa Jarmouni sings: 'Ayn Kirma bring me your news.' Ferghani sings about the garden, the well and the water wheel. 'Shaykh al-Kurdi, circumciser, do your thing! The knife sharpener is at his post, and the roving pedlars move like dark clouds from one place to another.'

This is the real heartland of the Constantinian! The place where he watches his own history pass him by, where he protects himself with his handicrafts against every intruder. It is the place where he launches his attack all the way east as far as the Sahara, with his silks and

---

1. Qur'an 22, 1–2. (I use Ahmed Ali's translation of Qur'anic passages [Princeton University Press, 1988] except where indicated otherwise.)
   Throughout the main body of the text, the notes are the translator's unless marked as 'author's note'.

copper, his perfumes and incense, his embroidered slippers and *kufiyyas*, even his candles and bridal kits.

Here is the Mosque of Sidi Lakhdar and over there the Mosque of Maimoun. The shrine of al-Masla is on the right and close-by the Mosque of the Bey. On the other side of the street is the Mosque of Sidi Qamoush.

The smells are overwhelming. The stench of rotting fruit and vegetables is enough to tear out your insides. The voice of the old townsman wearing the fez was ringing in his ears: 'They've sucked up all the air and left in its place the stench of their armpits.'

He commented to himself as his eyes wandered along the city walls:

The truth of the matter is that half a million people are just too many for this city. The walls look as though they're slanting. There's no doubt they're showing signs of fatigue. 'Every suckling female will forget her suckling, and every pregnant female will discharge her burden, and you will see men drunk, yet it will not be in intoxication. Indeed, God's punishment will be severe.'[1] God has spoken the truth.

A strange feeling came over him, and he felt a darkness within him that was turning into some kind of fluid, like gasoline or molten lead, something heavy melting in the heat. He hesitated for several moments before he decided to cross the small square and head towards the lane where once stood the famous Belbey Restaurant. He stared in a daze at the entrance to the restaurant and couldn't believe his eyes. It was the same restaurant, but my God, how much it had changed! He turned towards the café across the street and saw that it too was still there, although eerily in a shambles! He continued to stare. The Hotel de France, opening his mouth but without uttering the truth, was not as it used to be. The Hotel de France has turned into a rat-infested fleabag! He turned around and looked back at the restaurant.

Ah! There it is! And there is the Hotel Tunis above it. The grocery

---

1. The translation: 'Indeed, God's punishment will be severe' is my own.

that was built to serve the hotel is still across the street. I wonder what it's selling now. That sly Ibn Khaldoun. Poor Ibn Khaldoun, a creative writer but definitely not a historian!

He went down the stairs towards the right and found himself inside the restaurant. The paint on the walls was peeling, and all the chairs and nice round tables that used to be there were gone. They had been replaced with dilapidated wooden benches and metal shelves against the walls.

There is no power or strength save in God! Is this really the Belbey Restaurant that was frequented by aghas, pashas, shaykhs and all the upper class? Where wealthy landowners and cattle herders came to meet? 'That day you will see every suckling female forget her suckling, every pregnant female will discharge her burden, and you will see men drunk, yet it will not be in intoxication.' God has spoken the truth.

He felt a wave of heat surging within him and the viscous liquid increasing its pressure. His facial muscles started to tighten and the pupils of his eyes were dilated. His lips puffed out and his tongue stuck out of his mouth as his neck bent back and forth.

'Welcome! Please come in!'

He was startled by a voice that called out a feeble, half-hearted invitation for him to come in and sit down. He wondered if a dignified shaykh, dressed in a summer suit and shining black shoes, should lower himself to come in and sit down on a bench in front of a metal shelf, besides all those riff-raff, prickly pear vendors, porters and pickpockets, truck drivers and waiters from seedy cafés. Should he have a bite to eat, a scrap of bread with peppers fried two days ago, or an egg boiled last week, or perhaps a cup of sour yogurt milk mixed with flour?

He studied the shaykh who had extended the hesitant invitation and soon recognized him, an old man with a heavy beard, wearing a pair of small thick glasses and a soiled white skullcap. He had on a ripped shirt patched in the front, trousers fading at the seat, and a pair of worn-out leather slippers. He was a short man with a large head and a sunken chest.

It was indeed Belbey in the flesh, except that his black hair had turned grey and his bones were weighed down by the weight of a huge paunch. O God, how things change!

'Whom do I see here? Is it Hafsi Pasha?'

'No.'

'Ben Shanouf Pasha? Hajji Muhata?'

'What's wrong with you? Do you only remember pashas and aghas and collaborators with the French? Have you forgotten the men of learning, the pious and other such notables?'

'Ah, Shaykh Abdelmajid Boularwah! Welcome, welcome. I could never forget your voice.'

Shaykh Abdelmajid Boularwah leaned over and embraced him with condescension. Then he said:

'My good man, everybody has progressed, but you seem to have fallen behind!'

'The world, this treacherous, deceitful world we live in, Shaykh. Praise is to God alone, we must thank him for the good and the bad. God spoke the truth when he said: "We are certainly able to bring better people than they in their place; and they will not be able to thwart us."[1] Indeed, God has spoken the truth.'

Boularwah followed the shaykh inside, then lowered his head to complete under his breath the Qur'anic verse which his host had just begun:

'So leave them to their vain disputes and amusements till they meet their day of reckoning promised them, the day when they will come out of their graves in all haste as though rushing to their altars, eyes lowered, shame attending. That is the day they have been promised.'[2]

'God has spoken the truth,' he then said out loud. 'But after all, good health is the most important thing in life.'

'We thank God for all that he has given to us, good and bad. Please allow me to invite you to have something. My goodness, after such a long absence!'

---

1. Qur'an 70, 40–41.

2. Qur'an 70, 42–44

'That's correct. I left Constantine a long time ago. Seven years in Tunisia and nine years in the capital, Algiers!'

'Ah, you live in Algiers now! What do you do there? You must be working for the government?'

'God damn that government of atheists and heretics. God forbid! I'm working in education. I'm a headmaster.'

'Please, I beg you, do sit down.'

'I see that your restaurant has changed quite a bit.'

'Come with me to the back room. I'll grill some meat for you, or a lamb's head, whatever you like. I also have some milk that hasn't been tampered with that I've set aside for special guests like yourself. This is such a joyous occasion, a real blessing.'

Shaykh Boularwah's attention turned towards a picture hanging on the wall, and he went over to it to see who was in it. He was quite surprised when he discovered that it was Shaykh Ibn Badis surrounded by Shaykh Tebessi and Shaykh Ibrahimi.

Merchants, even those who have betrayed their countries or who have gone bankrupt, stand next to us, next to our venerated ancestors. These are the real people, not the labourers, sharecroppers and herdsmen.

He lapsed into thought, and then he turned towards Belbey whom he noticed was smiling joyously, and thought to himself: Finally, I've found someone whom I can identify with. These are the real pious people!

'Please come in!'

'Thank you. You're very kind.'

He stopped for a moment then went into the back room where his host offered him a seat. He asked him to wait a moment at a table that still maintained some semblance of refinement and which in fact looked luxurious in comparison to the stark benches and metal tables in the main dining room. As soon as his host left the room, he looked around to examine the walls. He noticed a large picture in a golden frame and stood up and went over to inspect it:

Belbey in all his splendour and glory, surrounded by an entourage of luminaries from all over the province of Constantine, pashas, aghas and military leaders, elected officials as well as senior government employees, glowing in the shimmering reflections of silver cutlery, crystal glasses and copper flowerpots.

Belbey returned with two bowls of soup, a large platter of grilled chops and a plate of fresh figs. He sat next to Boularwah.

'How are things in the capital?'

'Not very well. It's the same there as it is everywhere. Ibn Khaldoun left a sign . . . and you, here?'

'As you see, people are practically devouring one another.'

'What happened to your wonderful restaurant? What caused it to deteriorate so much?'

'Ah, let me tell you! The French left and the Muslims moved quickly to take their places. An apartment that used to house one family now houses several. French families counted no more than three or four members at the most. Today your cousins' families extend to at least nine or ten. Constantine has been overrun by bedouin from the villages and small towns. There's no one left to patronize fine restaurants or even modest ones, for that matter. Even when someone comes to town just to spend a night, or to visit his kid in school or buy a spare part, he has a relative he can drop in on and get a bite to eat. So I've been forced to survive in these conditions. I sell a few peppers, an egg or two, some milk, things like that. We must accept what is dealt to us from on high, both the good and the bad.'

'Today, the imam at the mosque gave a sermon about the earthquake.'

'You don't say! That imam is a bit too late! Constantine has already been struck by an earthquake, and that's that!'

'What are you saying?'

'The real Constantine is finished. I mean, it has already been struck by an earthquake. No one's left from the old days. Where is the Constantine of Belbey and Belfagoune, Ben Jaloul, Bel Tshikou and Ben Krara? There's already been an earthquake, it's come and gone, and Ben Finara and Ben Shair, Benfoul, Ben Tamin and every Ben so-and-so have arisen in its aftermath.'

'But this earthquake is really big, huge! It will bring everything down and put an end to the world, just as it says in the Qur'an.'

'The earthquake happens only once, my good Shaykh Boularwah. But there are those who feel it before it actually happens. Then there are those who feel it while it is happening, and those who feel it after it happens, eventually. The real earthquake is something everyone will feel.'

'Indeed, this is how God describes it in the Qur'an: "Every suckling female will forget her suckling, and every pregnant female will discharge her burden, and you will see men drunk, yet it will not be in intoxication." God has indeed spoken the truth.'

'Yes, he has spoken the truth! But you see, my good Shaykh Abdelmajid, I felt the earthquake the day the shepherds, the barefoot and the naked from the countryside came into town to kill off all the landlords. That's when I felt the real earthquake. How many pashas and aghas, civil and military leaders died at the hands of these sheep herders, sharecroppers, woodcutters and coal miners right in front of this very restaurant? "When the barefoot, the naked and the sheep herders build palaces and the servant gives birth to her mistress."[1] All of that did happen and it's all over. We accept what God gives us, both good and bad, and we thank him for good health.'

Shaykh Abdelmajid Boularwah ate voraciously and he spoke as though he didn't have a care in the world, only occasionally looking up to stare at his host.

This is not a real merchant, not at all. He's been influenced by the riff-raff who come and eat in his restaurant. He's become one of them. What a pity! The great Belbey, friend of aghas and pashas, scholars, judges and town officials, has been reduced to this!

'The day I had to fire all my help, I rolled up my sleeves and went to work. I've had to feed others before I was able to feed myself, my

---

1. This is a *hadith*, a saying attributed to the Prophet Muhammad, concerning what will happen at the hour of doom, cited in Ibn Kathir, *Alamat yawm al-qiyama* [The Signs of the Day of Judgement], ed. Abd al-Latif 'Ashur (Dar Bouslama, Tunis, 1983), pp. 141–2.

own children and their children as well. I've already felt the earthquake. Health is everything, my good Boularwah.'

Belbey was about to go on as though he guessed what his guest was
thinking, or perhaps he was only trying to convince himself. But
Boularwah began to mutter and abruptly cut him off:

'I've realized something. There isn't one merchant, one businessman who is content with himself, with other people or with the
situation as it is. People experience a sense of malaise. The masses are
suffocating. They feel great distress, a dark shadow and viscous liquid
filling their souls.'

'I feel like a jar that has been long broken. One day you're on top
of the world, the next day you're down and out. What else can we do
but accept our fate!'

Shaykh Abdelmajid Boularwah didn't allow his host to go on,
bothered as he was by his excessive complacency and contentment.

'Do you have any idea what brought me here in such unbearable
heat?'

'No.'

'I came to preempt them.'

'Who?'

'The government.'

'The government?'

'Yes, come closer. It's a secret. Only a few people know about it.
Listen. They're going to rob people of their property.'

'People's property?'

'They have this devious, dangerous plan. It's all very secretive.'

'What are you talking about?'

'They're going to confiscate land from the legal owners.'

'Confiscate land from the owners?'

'Yes. Listen to me. They're going to nationalize all private
property.'

'What are they going to do with it?'

'What they did with the lands that the French left behind. Can you imagine such spite and jealousy? They're really showing their true colours.'

'But you said that you came to preempt them?'

'Yes, but what I'm telling you must remain just between us. On the other hand, there's no problem if you alert property owners, big or small. What I intend to do, at least on paper, is divide my property among my heirs, so that if they come to confiscate it, they won't find very much in my possession.'

'But you've come too late, Shaykh Abdelmajid. This matter was taken care of years ago by these swindlers. It's been clear ever since they started talking about socialism.'

'To think that we in the capital believed that we were smarter than everyone else. We thought we knew what these politicians were up to. But it's obvious that we were deceived. You can't tame a jackal, Belbey.'

'That's for sure. So you came to divide your property among your sons. Then the matter seems quite simple.'

'Among my heirs. Unfortunately I don't have any children. But it's not as simple as you think . . .'

'How so?'

'First of all, I must track down my relatives. I haven't seen any of them since the war, in fact, well before that. I don't even know if they're alive or dead! Then I have to convince them to help me carry out my scheme. Finally, and this is extremely important, I have to take steps immediately. Word has it that we need to act quickly. They're going to make an announcement very soon.'

'You'll only have to find one or two relatives.'

'The problem is somewhat more complicated. It's a question of how much property there is. I own more than seven thousand acres.'

'Is that right?'

'Some of it I inherited, some I bought and some was forfeited to me by other heirs.'

'You may be too late, Shaykh Boularwah.'

'Who ever thought we'd end up like this?'

After the lunch there was an awkward moment as Belbey hesitated to accept payment for the meal and Shaykh Boularwah was equally hesitant about paying for it. But soon enough Belbey's son came into the back room and snatched the money from his hands.

'May God reward you and make you prosper,' he said, smiling.

Shaykh Abdelmajid Boularwah left the restaurant hurriedly and climbed the cobblestone stairs, surrounded by the pounding of the cobblers' tools, the stench of leather and human feet and armpits, and the aromas of perfume coming from the barber's shop to the right. He wondered how all these people could live and work together, one in his shop, the other in the doorway. Some of them made shoes, slippers and sandals, while others worked at repairing them. And then there were many who did both! Ah, here's something new, a radio and television repair man! He wasn't here when I left Constantine. Electricity and electrical appliances, radios and other such devices now exist even among the cobblers and prickly pear vendors.

As people went up and down the steps, hurrying about their business, a multitude of odours rushed forth in waves, each one very distinct from the other.

The women whose heads were exposed far outnumbered those covered in black veils. The eyes of these women, especially the young and unmarried, had a hungry look and their glances were full of curiosity and shameless flirting. It's obvious that marriage is at a standstill in Constantine. There's no place to live. 'The apartment that used to house one family now houses many . . .' It's also clear that life is topsy-turvy here in this town. Confusion has become the norm. The vendors all bump into each other, as do the merchants and craftsmen. Neighbours interact in shamefully open ways, while fathers and sons and brothers and sisters do not behave towards each other the way they used to. Pedestrians and cars cross the streets all at once, while the city's aromas and stenches blend together like the different accents, faces and sexes. The walls tilt, the roofs are caving in and there are half a million people sitting on top of the rock.

Ah, at last the Mosque of Sidi Qamoush. There is no power or strength save in God. From Him we come and to Him we return! The mosque has been occupied. They turned it into a private clinic for a lung specialist. God help us! 'The Earthquake of Doom is a tremendous thing. On that day you will see that every suckling female will forget her suckling, and every pregnant female will discharge her burden, and you will see men drunk, yet it will not be in intoxication.' ... The rock will bring us all down. Water will pour out in every direction. God only knows how violently the earth will split open and burst in explosions! At any moment the rock will announce in its own way that it is no longer able to support all of us. O, Sidi Rashid, man of miracles, pronounce your sentence. Remove from this rock these wicked, corrupt people ... The real earthquake is something everyone will feel. Why is it then that it has taken me so long to feel it myself? How is it that the feel for this earthquake to come has died in Belbey's soul in such an atmosphere?

When he reached the top of the stairs, he darted out onto 19 May 1956 Street where he suddenly felt the intensity of the midday heat. He could also feel the viscous fluid oozing within him, filling his insides with a thick darkness. His chest was tight and full, his head throbbing, and he felt faint. He stopped to lean his hands, elbows and back against the wall.

This used to be Avenue de France. It began where Avenue Caraman ended and where the Lycée Aumale was located.

This used to be a lover's lane, where the eyes of young European and Jewish girls sparkled with infatuation, joy and gaiety. Here you could always get a whiff of 'Jasmine' perfume, 'Rêve d'Or' and other intoxicating scents.

'We are certainly able to bring better people than they in their place; and they will not be able to thwart us.'

He continued on his way, hoping to find a café where he could sit down and rest a bit. But when he looked up ahead towards the causeway, he stopped. There were clouds of dust tumbling in the street and the spittle on the ground glistened in the sun. People were rushing about their business. Some of them carried turkeys, others baskets of eggs. Some were pushing small carts carrying crates of tomatoes, onions or prickly pears, and vendors of all kinds spread out in every direction. One person would grab something and another would pay for it. Above all, everyone was in a hurry.

As he bent his head towards the ground, looking down at his feet, he happened to overhear an old woman telling another a story in a distinctive rural accent. She had on her lap small rolls of hemp.

'I was with that poor abandoned woman that day. The sun was out but not as hot as it is today. She had her seventh kid on her back. You know, the father left them when the child was only four months old and took off for France. He promised to send her money as soon as he got there, but hasn't sent her a penny until now.'

'Maybe he hasn't found a job yet.'

'As I was saying, the poor thing was carrying her child tied to her back with an old wash cloth, while I carried her sixth kid who still wasn't walking. The sickle was in her hand and her chest was covered with a canvas vest. We were working on the estate of Hajj Boulabayiz who hired us for the summer and paid ten dinars for a bushel of wheat and two bushels of barley.

'So the little boy was sleeping on her back and sweat was pouring out from all over her body. She was breathing heavily. The sickle passed from one hand to the other as she snatched up the stalks of wheat. When she had gone a few steps towards the row of harvesters she suddenly screamed out: "Ah, my God, help me. My children are orphans."

'I ran towards her. So did all the others. Her whole leg had turned blue from the foot all the way up to her navel. Then her entire body turned blue. The poor thing, stricken by an evil genie!

'We bled her veins, we tried to give her the best treatment we could, but by night-time, she gasped her last breath. She left seven kids and they all clung to my apron-strings crying: "Nana, Nana!"'

Sidi M'sid
(The Sidi M'sid Bridge)

May God deprive you of His blessings, you old shrew!

Every new moon, the likes of you breed like rabbits. You give birth to insects and then complain about them. You populate the world with demons. You're the cause of all this upheaval and it's you who will bring on the earthquake!

Shaykh Boularwah muttered to himself as he crossed from one street to another. His immediate goal was the Bahjat Café where he could catch his breath, relax and leave behind the two old women and their stories of misery and gloom. As he was making his way towards the café, he passed the Monoprix supermarket and heard the voice of Ferghani singing along with a *rebab*:

'O, Sidi Talib, cure me of what ails me . . .'

The sign of the municipal clinic appeared before him. As he walked along the wall he saw a sign which read *No Parking* in both Arabic and French. No doubt, it had been there since the old days. Nevertheless, you could still find a line of cars parked all along the wall. 19 May 1956 Street was to the right, while Palestine Street ran straight ahead.

In the old days the Bahjat Café was a meeting place for the elite who came from miles around. It used to be the custom that whenever a stranger came in, he would soon hear a waiter whisper:

'Your drink has been paid for.'

'Who paid for it?'

'A Constantinian of pure stock who prefers to remain anonymous.'

The fervour of nationalism erupted here. It was here that the petty bourgeoisie came into its own.

And now?

There is no power or strength save in God. The sign still reads Bahjat, but the paint is faded and the sounds of backgammon chips have replaced the songs of Farid al-Atrash:[1]

'Flying carpet, gliding in the air, smooth and fair!'

Only sporadic traces of the old life remain. They destroyed one world and set up another. They pounced on the soul of Constantine, putting all their weight on the rock.

All those who were sitting down, and even the people passing by, bore the features of the rural Shawiya. How could they all cross the valley, the seven bridges, the narrow lanes and alleyways, and climb their way up to the kasbah and even to the outskirts of Constantine?

I wonder what is it that these people struggled for? Was it to leave their villages and mountains only to be crammed into Constantine? I should say not! My head is killing me. These backgammon chips are driving me out of my mind. This city air is suffocating me, not to mention all these people frantically coming and going. If it weren't for this urgent matter which has brought me here, I would leave this netherworld immediately. I wouldn't hesitate for one minute! There is nothing human left of this place except appearances. And even these, of streets, buildings and bridges, and perhaps a few names and addresses of cafés and other places, are fading away, submitting to pressures from above and erosion from below.

'Every suckling female will forget . . .'

'O man of miracles, shake these people and their perfidy from this rock . . .'

'They have sucked up all the air . . .'

'You can feel the earthquake, sooner or later . . .'

They have destroyed our city and have headed for the countryside to conspire against the pious servants of God.

---

1. Lebanese musician, singer and actor (d. 1974).

Ah! . . .

This thing is weighing heavily on my chest and running through my veins and nerves, paralysing my joints and muscles, crawling up towards my brain. I'll go to the edge of the rock and stand in the shade of an arch to catch a breath of fresh air which Sidi M'sid will so generously give me.

He lifted his head and right in front of him was a sign which read *Kharrab Sa'id Street*. He shook his head thinking how appropriately it was named, Kharrab, 'the destroyer'. Then he thought out loud in his mind:

Ibn Khaldoun will burn in hell forever for what he wrote, that it was the Arabs who brought the one, true, monotheistic religion, and that it is impossible that they symbolize the destruction of life. But the fact of the matter is that they not only destroyed life, they destroyed religion as well.

The Arabs build with one hand and destroy with the other.

On the contrary! Ibn Khaldoun is a liar. He is damned to hell! These are not Arabs, nor are they Berbers, nor Vandals nor Tatars, Mongols or Copts. They are either Russians whom God has sent to devastate the lands, or they are hordes of people without a race, religion or state. When we as Arabs, pure and free of mind, laboured to defend our Arabism and our religion, alongside Ibn Badis and his companions and disciples, men of nobility and learning, we did so as builders, not as destroyers. We spread the pure Arabic language, the language of the Qur'an, and we opened people's hearts to the traditions of the Prophet Muhammad and the sacred customs of our ancestors. But before we were able to accomplish our mission, they set fire to our lives. As soon as the French left, they destroyed the civilized populations of the cities, and now they set out for the countryside to exterminate what is left of noble and pious people.

He stopped. He placed his right hand on the wall. He bent his left knee and leaned over. Then he wiped the sweat from his forehead and sighed deeply.

I ask God's forgiveness. May the Devil be cursed. I have been overtaken with doubt and anxiety. The struggle is one thing. So is independence, colonialism and the law. But destruction, atheism and heresy, these are something else. May God look favourably upon this nation and bestow upon it another Ibn Badis and other noble men who will save us, even if a thousand earthquakes should strike us. May they continue what our sacred ancestors began but were prevented from completing because of the course of events!

He raised his head and looked straight out onto the street. The shop that sold shopping bags is still there as it has always been, but the one next to it no longer sells German radios. A barber's shop has opened there. The milk vendor is still there and he probably hasn't changed his fez in years. Mamy Isma'il used to live there. His bookstore and printing office used to be up ahead, at the top of the street. He used to publish *al-Najah*, which was the official newspaper of the local administration. He was an important and influential man who has most likely fallen out of favour, if he is not totally forgotten or dead. It was in his bookstore that all the government leaders and officials were chosen. And it was right there where important issues were decided. Now look at it! It's become a second-hand furniture shop. The signs on the printing press have either all faded or been dumped into the garbage.

He continued walking.

It seems that most of these people are from the Shawiya. Ah, here is the central barracks of the city. The walls of these floors tilt towards this side. This road leads down towards City Hall. There's the mayor's office and the centre of the city. The Jews used to control this area when it was full of shops. You used to hear the voices of the soldiers as they chatted up the giggling and squeaking young ladies. Yet the area is quiet now despite the crowds.

How strange it all is, how crowded all these shops are. Business is booming in spite of everything. Perhaps it's the incessant feeling of the earthquake that makes people rush out and spend their last dinar on anything in sight. It's as though they're looting in a mad rush against what little time they have left, like criminals sentenced to die. The feel of the earthquake escapes no one, neither those who are loved nor those who are despised.

As he was leaving Zirout Yusuf Street, which turns into Yugoslavia Street, he turned around and stared at the barracks.

That tilting seems a lot worse from here. It probably split down the middle and that's why the building slants in opposite directions.

He crossed the street and pressed his chest against a wall. He took a long, deep breath.

Finally, the smell of earth. Thank God. Finally, I can smell the earth. The city is like a boat stranded in the middle of the ocean. At every stop it evokes feelings of loneliness and alienation, of being cut off from the rest of the world.

From this side there is an eerie calm. They're trying to escape from confronting their fates. They're all afraid that if they stop or walk on the same side of the street, then the poor rock will lose its equilibrium.

He walked on a short distance and found himself on Yugoslavia Street. He wondered whatever possessed them to divide the street into two parts in this way, and to give one part the name of a martyred hero and the other the name of a communist country. The same thing exists in Algiers where there is a divided street, one part called Zirout and the other Che Guevara. At first we thought nothing of it, merely names. But now that the jackals have bared their teeth, we must take notice of every detail.

He hid beneath the shade of a passageway, and his eyes wandered towards the distant horizon.

The views of the mountain tops of endless shapes and sizes sometimes lose themselves in the whiteness of the clouds, and sometimes in the dark shadow of the trees. Ranges of hills crawl behind them towards the depression. Some are in full view, while others are totally stripped of any herbage save a few patches of green. At the foot of the mountain range, the green vegetation extends all along the right side and encircles the twists and turns of the river with its brackish waters and gleaming white rocks. All the way down below, there is a pier that stretches from the foot of the mountain and cuts across the river. This is the Sidi M'sid Bridge.

An old factory in a shambles stands towards the left. It looks as though it may have been a power station at one time. Although it is far away you can see beyond it, on a deserted road, a triangle of about a hundred hovels, all of them with mud walls and tiled roofs.

The Sidi M'sid quarter looks like the Garabi' quarter in Najib Mahfouz's novel, *The Children of the Alley*.[1] The Egyptians were too cowardly to kill Mahfouz for writing that trash, with all its heathen, heretical ideas and its mockery of our prophets and angels.

As the street climbs towards the left, it branches in two directions, one towards Constantine and the other towards Setif. Just beyond where the road forks, you can see a huge billow of bluish smoke rising above, as though it was coming from a volcano that erupted in many places and spread out over a vast area. This is the famous Boulfarayis dump. The breaks in the smoke looked like dark shadows that moved eerily in the sky, expanding then shrinking, appearing and disappearing, moving about left and right.

Several desolate hills separate this 'Bosphorus' from the village of Kudiya, which runs down along the slope. There you could find ramshackle buildings and overcrowded villas, surrounded by green trees and set among gardens which grow smaller and smaller as they get closer to the mass of hills. Then even more desolate hills stretch as far as the triangular quarter, on both sides, until you get to the bottom, the city of Awinat al-Foul.

On the top of this rock, criss-crossed with roads and tunnels, sits a city populated by half a million people and trod upon by vast numbers of cars and trucks. It is jam-packed with junk and loaded down with millions of tons of goods, hundreds of thousands of gas bottles, millions and millions of tons of lead and cement, canals and pipes. From time to time a bottle of gas explodes and a whole building crumbles into bits and pieces.

1. Controversial novel written in 1959 and recently retranslated into English by Peter Theroux (Doubleday, New York, 1996).

From here, from down below!

From this netherworld the water seeps out, and escaping in its every drop is a particle of earth and a fragment of this wretched rock.

From here, from Sidi M'sid, the destruction of the city will commence. It will only take one stone, as insignificant as it may appear, pulling free from this rocky wall that has been plastered over in more than one place. All of a sudden it will fall out and the rest will follow. The smaller cliffs and hollows will crumble and this huge slope will cave in.

From here, on the western bank, lies the great depression towards the west, extending all the way to the sea. There was and will always be a great danger to Constantine from this area. In fact, the West has always been the great threat to Arabs and Muslims, to their cities, their lives and their religions.

Oh, my head feels dizzy, my heart is beating fast and my knees are wobbling. Looking at this lower world, especially from this height, always makes you dizzy. I feel so sick and depressed.

'Indeed, the Earthquake of Doom is a tremendous thing... Every suckling female will forget her suckling, and every pregnant female will discharge her burden, and you will see men drunk, yet it will not be in intoxication.'

No, Sidi Rashid! Protect this rock, Sidi M'sid, as you have always done. Have mercy on the innocent, on the pious servants of God, on all the righteous and honourable people who still live on top of it. Rid it of the scoundrels who desecrate it with their filthy bodies and their licentious ways. Send 'hordes of chargers flying against them . . . pelting them with stones of porphyritic lava'.[1] Start here at the bottom where the earth still abounds; then move up to the heart of the city and purify it, O Sidi M'sid. Do not let them ruin the city lest they come and devastate the countryside. Render their menfolk impotent and their womenfolk sterile, so that their species becomes extinct, and only righteous people survive.

---

1. Qur'an 105, 3–4.

He turned away from where he was looking down below. He raised his head and stared once again at the municipal barracks.

They dug into this rock and built this road. On top of this steep slope they built the barracks and the rest of the city. They patched up the rock with cement in many places, and they covered up the holes by building walls cut from granite.

This premonition of the earthquake made them build these barracks, these roads and walls. But it only takes one slab of granite, or one chunk of cement, or one single stone to fall out of place, and the whole thing will come tumbling down! Whatever possessed the first man to come and settle here in such a dangerous place? Most likely it was in order to escape something even more dangerous. The first inhabitant of Constantine must have been a fugitive from justice, or maybe a vagabond highway robber who stole at night and took refuge here by day.

I am exhausted. My back is killing me and I feel overwhelmed by this viscous fluid weighing on my chest.

He turned down towards Zirout Yusuf Street and when he reached it, he stopped to think . . . They should put up a wall here like the Berlin Wall to keep everyone in his place . . . In front of him was a café from where he could hear the shouts of men playing backgammon and slamming down their chips. When he read the sign, *Café of High Spirits*, he muttered to himself: May God dampen your spirits!

He walked on, telling himself out loud that it was time to carry out his plan of action, while fixing his eyes on a row of whitewashed buildings. They were high-level administrative buildings. They'll be the first to fall when the earthquake strikes. Their important documents will blow away like dust all over Sidi M'sid.

'Have you ever seen or heard of such a thing?'

'What?'

'Look!'

'The bowling club, down below. That's the entrance. What of it?'

'It's empty. No one playing, no one sitting, no members.'

'So what of it?'

'That's the way it is, Tahir Ben Ali. Have you ever heard of a bowling club that doesn't sell alcohol?'

That's the way it is, Tahir Ben Ali. Every day one more café is prohibited from selling alcohol. So its owner and all the customers abandon it. People drink and people sell things to buy drinks and nobody thinks anything of it. And then the government officials try to curry favour with them by pretending to defend their morals and religious beliefs.

'Let them do whatever they want. They'll continue to drink until the Day of Judgement.'

'Let them drink arsenic!' yelled Shaykh Boularwah at two men who were passing by, without even looking at them. He continued walking. He felt as though he was no longer going down a hill. He looked ahead, saw a slight incline, then a huge decline.

Ah, that's La Brèche. I'll get something cold to drink, then go over my list of relatives to refresh my memory. I'll contact each one of them and not waste too much time wandering around in this infernal city.

His nose was assaulted by two very distinctive odours. He turned to the right. The smell of smoke was very strange. The Boulfarayis dump was burning with an eerie calm. The second odour was that of decay, of rotting fruit and vegetables from the market-place, which was coming from below the square. The loading carts were piling up, waiting to be emptied or filled. Just another sign that Constantine has ties to the outside world. Above the market is the main square with all its glimmering parasols, its many-coloured benches and its tables of odd shapes and sizes.

The square is teeming with passers-by who far outnumber those sitting down. Everywhere you look you find kiosks that sell cold drinks and ice cream. It's so embarrassing how they name them. It only shows how ignorant and exploitative the owners really are. There is *Sharia Ices*. I'll bet only one out of a million people, outside the population of Algeria, knows what the word actually means and that it is related to the Sharia Mountain; and it isn't even Sharia Tebessa which signifies snow or ice. Then there is *Iceberg Island*. Maybe it's named after some lake? But what does an iceberg have to do with a drawing of a Japanese deity set between the two words. *Siberian Ices*, now, that's reasonable, except that Siberia is now under communist rule. *Mont Blanc*, that's a name that we've inherited, no doubt. *Colliyya*, that must be named after the town of Collo. A blatant appeal to localism! If not, then what's the relation between the town of Collo by the sea and ices? They would have been better off naming the kiosk after one of the smaller villages, like Tamalous, Zitouna or Ain Keshra. *Welcome* reads the sign. Why didn't they just write *Come on in*? The *Ice Stars Café*. What does that mean? And then there are those who don't put any signs at all on their kiosks. Maybe they're afraid of getting involved with ice or icebergs, or of not being able to practise another trade if winter fails to come.

There is an isolated building that stands behind the square. It's the Palace of Justice screaming out to you that, whatever condition the city may be in, there is a power that rules over it. The building wants everyone to feel its presence. May they all be damned, whether by the dark of night or the light of day. None of them has any idea what justice means, these people who sit and plot how to take over other people's property.

There's the post office over on the left. The city is indeed linked to the outside world. If the rock starts to shake from the bottom up and the earth begins to quake, then the world will hear about it and come rushing to help the victims. But they won't find any survivors. This earthquake will be the most horrendous earthquake ever known. Truly devastating. 'Every suckling female will forget her suckling, and every pregnant female will discharge her burden, and you will see men drunk, yet it will not be in intoxication.' Buildings will come tumbling down, bottles of gas will explode and tongues of fire will shoot up in the sky.

Ah, there's something heavy weighing on my chest and head and running through my veins. I should never have allowed the spectre of the earthquake to haunt my mind and imagination. Everything is predestined, and we cannot go against God's wishes. Everything is in

His hands. God is indeed good, and indeed more just than all men. Let me have something cold to drink and I'll go down the list of relatives to see who could be my trusted heirs. Then I'll finish my business and be on my way.

The whole world is boiling, raging like a violent sea. Four streets swallow everything up and spit it all back out. Just like the main square! Wagons, long lines of trucks and carts waiting to be loaded and unloaded. Hand carts push crates of fruits and vegetables. Old men, old women, children rushing down towards Sidi M'sid or Hama.

'They will come out of the graves in all haste as though rushing to their altars.' Indeed, God has spoken the truth.

On the Day of Resurrection, the man on the beast will appear. The tail of the beast will be in the east, and its head in the west. The beast will be pulling a large cauldron seven times the size of the earth, full of boiling water. The man on the beast will stretch out his hand and seize all the evildoers and throw them into the pot.

Begin here, man on the beast, and start with all these newcomers to Constantine, those who weigh it down and will cause an earthquake. Start with all those who corrupt our religion with heresies.

God forgive me! These are the mad ramblings of old women which should not be invading my thoughts.

'Would you like to buy something, uncle?'

He turned around and saw a young man of sixteen, wearing a tattered blue jacket and carrying several heads of lettuce tied to a bamboo cane. He stared at him closely without responding to the question.

'Are you buying anything, brother?'

This time he was asked the question by an old man who was carrying a cardboard box filled with plastic packets of herbal concoctions. They actually sell herbal teas in the summer. I guess anything goes in this city of contradictions.

'Why don't you buy something from me, so that I can get rid of all these packets and buy something to eat for myself and the missus? Today I decided that if I earned three dinars, I'd buy myself a razor to shave with. I just threw away the old one I used for six months. It got so that you couldn't even cut butter with it.'

'Today is Friday. All ye faithful, give alms to the poor!' cried a middle-aged blind woman who had a colourful bath towel wrapped around her shoulders.

She's a Jew, I'm sure of that. Her tribesmen who could see have all taken off and she has no idea in which direction they went.

'Welcome, welcome! What a pleasant surprise!'

The greeting, coming from an older man dressed in a pyjama top and wearing nothing on his head, overwhelmed him. He was cleanly shaven, but with dirty trousers and muddy feet. Not content to merely shake hands, he embraced Shaykh Boularwah warmly.

'You don't seem to remember me! Don't you remember me at all? Ah, I'm sure it's you. Well anyway, I'm certain that you're coming from the capital. I'm Ammar, the mason. I was in Bouzareah, Anasir, Belcourt and Hussein Dey. I met you. I saw you there. I'm now living in Constantine and life is hard, as you can see. I used to work at the Prince Abdelqadir Mosque. Then some problems arose and they threw me in jail. Please allow me to offer you a coffee. It's on me. If I had more money, I'd offer you something nicer. At any rate, I want to ask you something. I live nearby with my wife, daughters and sister-in-law. To tell you the truth, I'm out of work and I need a little cooking oil. Why don't you come and have some coffee at my house? My wife, daughters and sister-in-law will be very happy. One of my daughters is twenty, another nineteen and the third seventeen. My sister-in-law is only twenty-two. What can we do, my brother? These are life's demands. The doctor wants his due, so does the pharmacist. A chair here, a pair of shoes, a light bulb, a bottle of gas, bread, salt, oil! Where does it end? Please allow me to buy you a cup of coffee!'

Shaykh Boularwah was dumbfounded as he listened to Ammar the mason expose his whole life to him in rapid detail. When he tried to take Shaykh Boularwah by the hand, he pulled back and yelled:

'What are you saying? Who are you?'

'The coffee's on me, it's my treat. Come to my house and let my daughters, wife and sister-in-law enjoy your company.'

'Get away from me, you despicable man, you son of a bitch, you pimp. You dare to say such a thing to me? There is no power or strength except in God! You're asking me, a sixty-year-old gentleman, one who has memorized the Qur'an, a graduate of the venerable Zaytouna Mosque, you're asking me to do such a thing and in this noble city of Ibn Badis, on a Friday no less? May you all be damned.

'Oh, Sidi M'sid, quickly, shake them all off this rock, them and their iniquity.'

People started to gather around Shaykh Boularwah while Ammar the mason slipped through the crowd, with his hands in his jacket pockets and a baffled look on his face.

'The Earthquake of Doom is a horrendous thing. Every suckling female will forget her suckling, you will see men drunk, yet it will not be in intoxication, people will come out of the graves in all haste . . . eyes lowered, shame attending.' The tail of the beast will be in the east, and its head in the west. It will be carrying a cauldron of boiling water with steam rising from it, while the man on the beast lifts a handful of these wretched people and throws them into the cauldron. He will not choose, he will not make exceptions, for they are all sinners, heretics and accomplices in evil.

That viscous fluid is oozing in my heart. I feel a deep depression and my throat is all choked up. The earth is shaking.

He stole away quietly from the crowd of onlookers who had gathered around him. He hurried towards the square, his feet tripping over each other and his stomach and buttocks jiggling. His head lolled around, at times in half circles, and at other times in full circles. His arms dangled as the sweat rolled down his face. His anger was so fierce it made his muscles twitch in spasms.

He headed towards the other end of the square and took cover under an awning made from embroidered cloth. He faced westward and fixed his gaze beyond the hills, past the Boulfarayis dump, as the smell of its smoke filled his lungs and the stench of the rotting fruit and vegetables from the souk poisoned his mood.

He tried to go on, to free himself of everything around him. He tried not to think about the city and its problems, or about the government and its atrocities, or the earthquake and the man on the beast.

Over there the Atlas Mountains extend all the way to the Mitija Plains. If the government wants to give people some land, then it should raze these mountains and divide the land among them. What good is it to be friends with the Russians if they can't level the mountains and build dams on them?

God made these mountains as pillars to fortify the land.

Let's open up the road so they can emigrate to France and the rest of Europe!

Let's sterilize the men and women so they stop breeding like rabbits!

This is an abomination!

But isn't it worse what we do every day and night and allow to continue to happen?

'What will you have, uncle?'

He was aroused from his depressing daydreaming and lifted his heavy eyes towards the waiter.

'A chocolate milk shake,' he muttered after a moment of dead silence.

'We only have ice cream and cold drinks.'

'Bring me some ice cream and a glass of cold water. Thank you!'

A sound that was all too familiar to him caught his attention and he looked in its direction to be certain . . .

The backgammon chips, even here! Damn you, Ibn Khaldoun, a thousand curses be upon you. This is a place to calm the nerves, to catch a breath of fresh air and to soothe the throat, not a place to play games. They never let go of these damn chips, even when the rock shakes and starts to dissolve. How did these stupid games get here? Who are these people sitting here? Who is responsible for changing

Belbey's luxurious restaurant into the dive that it is today? They've taken over every inch of the city and transformed it into their rural, backwater towns. They've set up a village in every corner of Constantine. They have no connections with one another except for buying and selling. It doesn't bother any of them that they're living the same way they did in the village. It's all the same to them, here or there. Everything around them, the grand monuments and the glories of Constantine, looks all the same to them. This is why the city people despise them. I wouldn't set one foot in this city built on such an unstable rock were it not for the important matter that has to be taken care of. O God, I must hurry up and go over my list of relatives who may still be alive and see who can be trusted to help me out in my plan.

He took out his pen and notebook and leafed through its little pages until he came across a page partly scribbled with figures for annual entries to his land, monthly receipts of rent, and prices for seed which he had paid over the last four years. He stared out into space for a moment, trying to remember the name of a relative. Failing to do so, he went back to reading the tiny numbers and letters scribbled on the upper half of the page.

The price of four medium-sized batteries for the radio, an additional expense for the month of July.

He went on thinking.

The first one who comes to mind is my brother-in-law, my wife's only brother. Ah, what's his name? Haven't seen him in nineteen years. The last time was when he came to see me looking for a loan of ten thousand old francs. He told me he needed to buy equipment for a barber's shop. He decided to be a barber and open up a shop on the sidewalk of the main boulevard. He was going to set up a table and chair between two cafés and put his trust in God like everyone else. I picked up my walking stick and yelled at him.

'Listen, isn't it enough that I feed your sister? I never want to see you here again. Get away from me! You only bring bad luck!'

The young man of twenty had turned bright red, visibly upset. He lowered his head and walked out.

'That's my brother. Shame on you!' yelled his sister.

'It's a shame to steal. It's a shame to covet someone else's property. Why doesn't he join the French army?'

Now I remember! Ammar, his name is Ammar. He came to me some time later and told me he was a barber on the sidewalk. But after the war broke out, I never heard from him again. I never knew what happened to him. Ammar is a barber on the street.

He started to jot something down.

I'll put him at the top of the list. I think he's probably forgotten that little incident and doesn't hold any grudge against me. But why hasn't he got in touch with me all these years? He's even forgotten his own sister! Even if he doesn't ask for a loan, I'll lend him fifty dinars. I'll give them to him as a gift, as an act of charity for the way I treated him the last time. After all, I was a bit hard on him.

He lapsed into a long daze, racking his brains to remember. His cousin came to mind.

His name is on the tip of my tongue. He used to call me 'uncle'. He took me by the hand, of course that was thirty years ago, and brought me to a café in Bardo. He sat me down and ordered me a tea.

'Listen, uncle. I need to ask your advice and seek your help at the same time.'

'If it's got anything to do with money, I don't want to hear it!'

'Listen to me first. Look at that store across the street.'

'Yes, that's a shop where they sell sieves. I know the owner. What about it?'

'It's for sale.'

'So what does that have to do with me?'

'They're asking for one hundred and fifty thousand francs.'

'For complete ownership?'

'No, for a licence to operate the shop, and twenty dinars a month for rent.'

'And what would I do with a sieve shop?'

'You can lend me that amount until next summer. I'll pay you back half what I make on the harvest. And the other half I'll pay you back in monthly instalments.'

'What assurance do I have to protect my money?'

'We're cousins, we don't need anything like that!'

'The hand of fate strikes every day. Who knows who will die and who will live?'

'We'll draw up an agreement.'

'That's not enough. Should you go bankrupt, your going to prison is not going to bring back my money.'

'I own land. Don't forget that, uncle. Had it not been for the expenses in building a house in the village, I would not be asking for such a loan.'

'You could mortgage your land.'

'Have we come to this, uncle?'

'One has to protect oneself, think about life and death, bankruptcy and success.'

'Then I'll mortgage half my land.'

'In that case I'll give you double what you're asking, three hundred thousand.'

He thought about it for a moment, took a deep breath and walked with me to the notary.

It just so happened that it was a lean year all over the country. The harvest was disappointing and people were not buying sieves. I put pressure on my cousin. I contacted the local authorities and people with connections and I recouped my losses. The magistrate came with the police and expelled him from the land, two hundred and fifty acres of good land, half of it arable. He tried to reclaim it the next year, but the process was not exactly child's play.

He was successful in his business, so he didn't die of starvation. At any rate, I can't imagine him still holding a grudge against me. We're family! Besides, what we lost in some ways, we gained in others. After all, we're all in this together.

He remembered his name. Abdelqadir!

I should write '*Caution, Beware*' beside his name, just in case he still bears a grudge and has it in for me. You can never be too careful. What will I do if he demands that I give him back his land? No! That's nonsense. He wouldn't do such a childish thing. The matter is over and done with. I'll put it in writing that I am going to leave a part of my land to him, of course, on condition that he receive it only after I die, and that he not sell or mortgage it to anyone outside the family. Let's not forget the saying: *When you divorce your wife, do not suggest a new husband to her!* But I must proceed cautiously. He lost his land once and he could do it again. After all, it's my land we're talking about, and even after I'm dead, I'll know what's happening to it.

God forgive me. The land is His! It is He who bequeaths it to His pious servants.

'Hey, uncle, how about a brushing or a shine for your shoes?'

'No, get away from me. Leave me alone!' responded Shaykh Boularwah to a barefoot thirteen-year-old, who was wearing torn jeans and a shabby T-shirt with a picture of Che Guevara on both the front and back. He was a rather handsome young man with blue eyes and long shining blond hair.

If that were my son I would dress him in fine linen and silk brocade. I'd have him live in palaces and marry him off to seven women and twenty slave girls. I'd give him all my land so that the government couldn't get its greedy hands on it. What a shame! The winds don't always blow in favourable directions, as they say. You sometimes find in the river what you cannot find in the sea; and you find in the swamp what you don't find in a river.

'Just one dinar, uncle, for a nice, professional job,' said the boy repeating his offer.

Shaykh Boularwah smiled faintly but then quickly bared his teeth and flew into a rage when the youngster came closer to him.

'May God wipe you off the face of the earth, you son of filth and shame. Get away from me!'

The young boy drew back quickly when he saw Shaykh Boularwah's face changing colour, his muscles quivering in angry convulsions and sparks of rage flying from his eyes. He moved back several yards and then he stopped. He wanted to make sure what he saw and heard was really happening. Was all this anger merely because he asked to shine his shoes? Lord help us, he thought, if this is what all my clients were like, we'd all die of starvation. He stared closely at the shaykh.

'God forgive me!' murmured Shaykh Boularwah. What did this poor kid do to deserve all my wrath? He's such a beautiful young man, exceptionally beautiful!

Then he smiled a fleeting but sincere smile. He pictured the young man in silk brocade, wearing a red velvet fez, shining red shoes and a bow tie around his neck, carrying a leather satchel and wearing a gold watch on his wrist.

Truly a child to cherish!

After years of waiting and dreaming here he was, now right before his very eyes, like something come down from heaven, complete, total, lacking for nothing, dressed in silk brocade, living in a palace with wives, pleasured by twenty slave girls, basking in the good life.

And the government not getting its greedy hands on my land!

The young boy was taken in by the smile. He came back and drew closer. He put his shoeshine case in his hand without uttering a word. The shaykh watched him closely, then whispered to him.

'What does your father do, my fine young man?'

'My father died in the forest! He downed a plane, killed a general and died in the forest. A burst of fire from a plane severed his legs and he shot it down. He kept fighting the enemy soldiers until a shell fell on his head and he died in the forest. My mother married a coal miner who was arrested by the forest rangers for lighting some firewood. They put him in prison and never let him out. I live with my grandmother and aunt. My aunt gets married every night. Each one leaves her five dinars then disappears without ever coming back. A good shine for your shoes, sir? It's only a dinar.'

'Get out of here, you little bastard! God damn you, your mother, your grandmother, your aunt and your government.'

However the youngster persisted and found a dirty pair of shoes on the table next to where the shaykh was sitting. Neither the shaykh nor the shoes' owner was able to get rid of him.

The shaykh went back to working on the list of his relatives.

Ah, I almost forgot. He had already memorized the Qur'an by the time he was fourteen. At the mosque he studied the *Ajurrumiyya*[1] and the *Risala*.[2] Then he became an ascetic and declared himself a devotee of the Shadhiliyya order of mystics, shutting himself off from the rest of the world to learn the Qur'anic sciences, write incantations and receive offerings. He's my cousin Issa on my mother's side. He probably doesn't know me, and even if he did, no doubt he won't remember me. He was eighteen when I left. He's someone whom I can trust. He must be one of the trustworthy. Who better than an ascetic? What this twentieth century of ours lacks is piety. I'll put a third of my land in his name. There was never anything between us except for the fact that I annexed his land with his mother's consent without his ever knowing. She died soon thereafter. She was always so depressed! I remember we used to fight all the time with the mosque attendants, the leaders of the orders and other such superstitious people, but I always thought they were better than these hard-hearted heathen infidels who are now running our government, even though Ibn Badis himself was always ready to attack them.

Then Issa it is!

He wrote down his name and next to it he jotted 'trustworthy'. He then went on to think hard, trying to remember.

Rizqi, the saddler, is also family. He's my father's cousin and a decent fellow. He minds his own business, even though he has a penchant for liquor and young men. There's really no problem to speak of between us. I married his sister, then divorced her after three years. He's undoubtedly forgotten such a minor incident. If his sister is still alive and not remarried, I'll even put a piece of land in her

---

1. A primer of classical Arabic grammar compiled by Ibn Ajurrum (d. 1323).
2. A treatise on the elements of Islamic law according to the Maliki school.

name. Of course, I'll do so on condition that she never remarry. If she wants to come back home, I'll even allow that. Whatever amount of food can feed two mouths can feed three. Perhaps Rizqi has sons whose names I can add to my list. The more names I can add to my legal heirs, the less the government will see of my property.

'For the sake of God, my dear faithful!'

'God will help you,' he replied to the beggar, without even bothering to lift up his head. He continued jogging his memory.

'Robber, grab that robber! He snatched my wallet and ran away. Catch him!'

A loud voice erupted close to where Shaykh Abdelmajid Boularwah was seated, quickly followed by the rattle of falling metal chairs and pounding footsteps. People gathered around and started talking in high-pitched voices, shouting for the thief to be caught.

'A hundred dinars', yelled the owner of the stolen wallet as he slapped the sides of his face in despair. 'My whole month's salary, money for my children's bread. Help me, brothers! Catch that thief.'

'Go to the police station! There they'll look for the man who stole your money,' urged a man standing in the crowd.

'God lets the tree grow and flourish, but He's not the one who cuts it down,' chimed in another.

As soon as all the commotion died down and things went back to normal, Shaykh Boularwah lowered his head.

Even that scoundrel cousin of mine, Tahir, I'll have to write down his name as well. He became a bum as soon as his father died. He spent four years in the French army and three in jail. He got out only to become a pickpocket at Camels' Square. He sold me his father's share of the land, with no regrets at all! He got into the habit of marrying and divorcing, as well as getting drunk, stealing and landing in jail. Either they've killed him or given him a life sentence, or he's still loafing at Camels' Square.

Tahir.

He wrote down his name, and added next to it a question mark and drew a circle around it. He put his address book in his pocket and took out his watch.

It's two o'clock. It's time to act. And there's that putrid odour which is getting worse and worse.

He started to get up but, captivated by the voice of a man sitting next to him telling a strange story, he sat down again and strained to listen with all the energy he could muster.

'It happened yesterday at the Boulfarayis dump. You can see the dump from here, there in front of us. You can even see the billows of smoke.'

'Yeah, I see it, they're really puffing up in the air.'

'The news came late, but I was able to save what I could.'

'What really did happen?'

'One of the municipal trucks was carrying jars of spoiled goods confiscated from a few stores. As soon as it dumped its load, all hell broke loose.'

'What do you mean, all hell broke loose?'

'All year long hordes of people who live in the caves, old people, middle-aged, youngsters, men and women, swarm around the Boulfarayis dump and rummage through the garbage. They pick out bones that people throw away and make soup out of them. It's a whole other world out there, with its own network of merchants, middle-men and gang leaders. They have their own laws and security system, set up by people who don't even wear shoes.'

'All that at Boulfarayis dump?'

'That's right, only some two and a half miles from here. Over there, look at all those shadows moving through the haze.'

'But what happened yesterday?'

'Oh yeah. All hell broke loose. They dived on the cartons, kicking and punching one another. The bosses and middle-men tried to stop the riff-raff, but it was no use. It got so out of hand that it turned into a brawl, and they had to use rocks, then sticks and finally daggers and rifles.'

'Even rifles?'

'Yes, anything. Bosses are bosses, right? Anyway, when we got there, we found twenty dead and seventy wounded.'

'All in good time, Tahir Ben Ali.'

'All in good time, Tahir Ben Ali.'

'Sometimes that's the way life is, Tahir Ben Ali.'

Sidi Rashid
(The Bridge at Sidi Rashid)

May God dispose of them all. May He dump you all, ashes in a heap of garbage a million times bigger than the Boulfarayis dump, where you'll rot in hell forever.

Shaykh Abdelmajid Boularwah thought to himself as he got up to flee from the two men rattling about the recent events at the dump.

He worked his way through the tables and chairs and found himself at a crossroads. To his left was Zirout Yusuf Street and beyond that a street whose name he didn't recall. Then there was 19 May 1956 Street, formerly Avenue de France. Next came Larbi Ben M'hidi Street, followed by the back alleys of Sidi Rashid. Directly to his right was the slope that headed down towards Martyrs' Square, followed by a network of smaller roads that went up and down, east and west, in fact, in all directions.

These streets are more important to Constantine than all of its buildings, public and private put together. Look at these people, walking around like zombies, as though they were trapped in a prison or a concentration camp. What would become of them if the city didn't open up all these arteries, even if they're all narrow and winding? When the earthquake comes, these roads and squares will be reduced to nothing but rows of pits and trenches.

No, I can't be thinking about the earthquake now!

He found himself surrounded by an entourage of odours, getting a whiff of grilled sweetbreads, then of burning prickly pear rinds. He could smell the stench of urine, mixed with chemicals and perfume. Of course there was the pervasive odour of armpits along with the stench of smelly feet. The right shoulder of one of the passers-by bumped him on his left side. He tried to move forward but found his way blocked.

'Pardon me, sir.'

A woman covered in black from head to toe asked to pass by, poking him in the stomach. He followed her with his eyes, amazed at her brashness. Someone stepped on his toe and he quickly pulled it away. He felt pain, annoyance and suffocation. You've got to be trained to walk in Constantine. They should send in technicians the way they send astronauts to the moon.

Before I plunge into Sidi Rashid, I'll stop off at the arcade to see my brother-in-law, Ammar. Maybe he turned his little work-stall into a real shop. Maybe he made some money and bought himself a nice barber's shop. Who knows, maybe he hit the jackpot after independence and managed to buy himself a luxurious boutique!

All this is part of Sidi Rashid, the real Constantine.

Ah, the Hotel de Paris! The grand hotel with three elegant cafés that overlook the square. This was the major rendezvous spot. Senior officials, landowners, contractors, aghas and pashas. High-powered businessmen and merchants. Entry to these places used to be strictly forbidden to the riff-raff. It was sheer shame that kept all the nobodies out! Rich satin-brocaded draperies flapped in the breeze and the fragrance of Parisian perfume filled the air. The waiters wore suits and uniforms more luxuriously decorated than those of the highest military officers.

'Would you care to buy something, uncle?'

He stared intently at the goods laid out in front of him and was soon accosted by an outstretched arm waving a turkey. He stepped aside so that he wouldn't get his suit soiled. He contemptuously stuck up his nose and forced his way ahead to avoid the turkey and its vendor.

'For you, a special price, practically for nothing. What do you say?'

He was tempted by the offer and looked up. It was a display of alfalfa brooms in every imaginable size. The oppressive heat took possession of his entire body. He felt as though he were suffocating and his body was growing limp. He felt a tremendous weight on his chest and that viscous liquid was oozing slowly inside him.

When the earthquake strikes, this entire square will become one large sewer that will stretch all the way to Sidi M'sid north-west and Sidi Rashid south-east. Every suckling female will forget her suckling, pregnant women will miscarry and nausea will afflict mankind. The man on the beast will be forced to carry away its wicked citizens, each and every one of them to the last infant, when he passes through the city. He'll even have to carry the buildings, everything from high-rises to shacks.

He'll scoop up Constantine with one hand.

As he approached Ben M'hidi Street, the smells of food on the right grew stronger as they blended in with the stench of urine. There were grilled sweetmeats, fried peppers, boiled eggs, shish kebabs and *meloukhia*. He detected the smell of boiling potatoes, grilled ground lamb and the overwhelmingly pungent smell of stale, dried urine. That disgusting combination of filth and stench!

These cafés have become hang-outs for all the different vendors and craftsmen. One thing that hasn't changed in this area are the hordes of shoeshine boys and newspaper vendors. In fact, nothing has changed, except that there are a lot more of them!

A half-million residents in one city, perched on a rock. What in God's name brought them all here? You would think it was an industrial town, but it isn't. It isn't even an important commercial centre or a cultural Mecca. With Ibn Badis' passing and our own excesses, neither culture nor knowledge now exists in Constantine. I could understand if they went to Annaba or Skikda, or maybe to Algiers or Oran, or even Marseilles or Belgium, that I could see. But their coming here is beyond me, unless they came to hasten the doom of this city with their filth, corruption and depravity.

Shaykh Boularwah was able to keep out of the way of both cars and pedestrians as he entered Ben M'hidi Street. He was content to let his legs carry him in the right direction.

If I don't find him, I'll be sure to find someone who knows him. People in the main streets may change, as do shops and businesses, but those in the back alleys, the hovels and the arcades always stay the same. If it weren't like that, you would never be able to locate the whereabouts of any of its merchants. Just look at Belbey, a classic example! He's like the last remaining tooth in the mouth of an old woman, witness to her once full set of teeth and attractive, radiant face.

He muttered to himself, feeling mixed emotions, thinking jumbled thoughts, all running amok through his head and heart.

Very nice, indeed! If this rock does quake, it will rid itself of everyone on it and the government won't have anyone to give land to. But it's really not their fault. They did well by escaping from the countryside and the small villages. Now there's no one left in any of the rural areas who wants land. And that will be the one major obstacle in the government's plan to violate the eternal divine order.

Their gravest sin was to congregate here in the cities where the government can keep an eye on them day and night, instead of staying in the mountains and canyons. But only a fearsome earthquake can redeem such a sin. The fault is absolutely the government's as long as it is unable to build enough factories. And why does it block the doors to Europe by placing obstacles in front of those who want to emigrate?

God in His infinite wisdom didn't create death, wars, flooding, earthquakes, plague and disease without a reason. Nothing escapes Him. If the rock fails to shake up this city, then everything will end up in Boulfarayis dump, where dogs and cats and people and rats will kick and claw at one another.

There are so many people.

They proliferate in frightening numbers. They're coming out of the walls, and will continue like that forever. Naturally, they proliferate. The government forces doctors to treat the riff-raff at low cost. They even make it easy for sharecroppers to receive medical treatment with social security funds; and they pick up all the costs! Why shouldn't these people proliferate so long as they eat and drink without working for it. And if they get sick, they get treatment by paying a paltry sum. They steal from the rich to waste money on the filthy, the naked and the sheep herders.

You can pour out of a vessel only what is in it! May God have no mercy on you, Ibn Khaldoun!

When Shaykh Boularwah stood at the entrance to the arcade, he could feel his eyes wandering and his thoughts rambling, as time turned upside down. There were sheep, cow and horse herders dressed in their black shirts standing all around him. There were also wealthy landowners and farmers in their black and white burnouses, in camel-hair coats, with yellow satin turbans tied with strips of camel-hair. Successful middle-men and businessmen wearing grey capes and red fezzes mingled in the crowds. In the middle of it all, old Idir, lord of the land and possessor of great wealth, emperor of Othmaniyya and Constantine, sat majestically, looking as though he were mounted on a throne.

'Good afternoon, Uncle Idir.'

'Good afternoon, Knower of Evil.'

'What makes you say "Knower of Evil"?'

'Knowledge and wealth do not mix. What did you have for lunch?'

'A quarter of a sheep's head.'

'A quarter of sheep's head and you come here to borrow money. Look at me! I am the emperor of Constantine and Othmaniyya, and I only had some yogurt. Lucky for you that you didn't have a whole sheep's head, then you wouldn't qualify for any assistance.'

'I know that you don't disappoint those who come to you.'

'That's part of my job. I do lend, but at ten per cent interest. Land is the usual collateral. Can I ask you what you intend to do with my money?'

'Despite my connection to wealth, Uncle Idir, the honourable knowledge that I serve prevents me from lying. If you must know, then I will tell you.'

'Even though I trust you and even with land as collateral, it would be nice to know what becomes of my money.'

'The truth is, Uncle Idir, I lend it at twenty per cent interest.'

'Ah, the big fish eats the little fish! The olive comes from the olive tree and the fish from the sea. You do indeed deserve the money. Come back a little later and you'll find the amount ready.'

'Thank you very much, Uncle Idir.'

'No need to thank me, Boularwah, I'm only doing my job. Besides, it's a shame not to buy and sell. By the way, how's your friend?'

'He's still busy writing a commentary on the Qur'an.'

'Tell him, Idir says to get rid of Belhamilawi[1] or else I'll throw him off the Kaf Shakara cliff.'[2]

Shaykh Abdelmajid Boularwah's mind snapped to attention. He opened his eyes and fixed them intensely on what was around him.

Twenty-eight years have passed since that incident. God have mercy on Shaykh Idir. He was such a practical man, so much so that anyone who had any dealings with him could only wish him more wealth and prosperity. I wonder who's taken over the arcade. What's all this I see in front of me? Who are all these people? Why is everyone wearing yellow turbans? They're all so clean shaven and dressed in white. They all seem so cheerful, even the old men. I wouldn't be surprised if some tiny hamlet from Milia, Jijel or Tahir has dumped all its people onto the arcade! Or maybe one of the town's prominent citizens is throwing a wedding and is requesting that his guests come dressed alike.

Such heathen practices abound. That wicked Ibn Khaldoun is more a writer of fiction than he is of history.

At the far end of the arcade is the bathhouse. There's a barber in his shop and another who sits at a table outside his door. Both are engrossed in their work, minding their own business. There are three cafés that operate harmoniously with one another as though they were all one big café. They even share the same tables and chairs. Two customers, with armloads of caftans by their side, sit between two cafés, drinking coffee together.

---

1. The shaykh of a mosque–shrine at the time of colonial rule [*author's note*].
2. A steep cliff in Constantine and the site of many local legends [*author's note*].

The Day of Judgement, the Earthquake of Doom, is when 'every suckling female will forget her suckling, and every pregnant female will discharge her burden, and you will see men drunk, yet it will not be in intoxication', when the wolf reconciles with the lamb, and the cat with the mouse, and the lion with man, as will every man with his enemy, when all oppositions come together.

Who are all these people dressed alike who differ only in their facial features, their ages and height?

'I want a music group tonight,' said a middle-aged man in an elegant European suit.

'What's the occasion?' asked a spry old man.

'A celebration!'

'I know it's a celebration! We only perform at celebrations.'

'A circumcision.'

'Congratulations. Unfortunately, no one can go to you before six o'clock.'

'Why so?'

'Because we have union elections. Either after six or tomorrow.'

'But . . .?'

'It's tough luck. We can't do everything at once.'

That viscous liquid suddenly receded in Shaykh Boularwah's chest, but then flowed out with sudden amazing speed. He felt a shiver shake his whole body, then a fever took hold of him. His teeth chattered and he clenched his fists. He felt an urgent need to sit down, to throw himself into the empty chair in front of him. He resigned himself totally to the stares that devoured him, astonished by his assault on their world!

'We are certainly able to bring better people than they in their place; and they will not be able to thwart us.'

The earth at Constantine has been trembling for some time. The earthquake is a premonition of fear, confusion and drunkenness, when the barefoot and naked sheep herders build palaces and the servant gives birth to her mistress.

The man on the beast won't have to throw them into his cauldron.

He'll ask Almighty God to turn Constantine into a huge cauldron that will be brought to a boil by seven suns, whose waters are seven seas that will boil so hot that their vapours will rise to the seven heavens. Then the citizens of Constantine will throw themselves into it to repent of their wicked ways. They chased away all the merchants whose noble profession received the blessings of our Prophet, and they replaced them with these honky-tonk flautists and tambour-players.

O hell! Open your gates and swallow up these people. Make them your eternal flames.

That wasn't enough for them. They brought in pinko-communism and organized unions for the masses. Unions against whom? Against life itself! God, you're too kind, too merciful.

Where are you now, Uncle Idir? With sacks full of gold and silver, you were content with eating only yogurt for lunch and dates for supper. Your riches were proverbial, your power legendary!

Where are all of you, you who drove the flocks of sheep with your sticks from the arcade on the boulevard in this radiant city of Constantine?

O, Sidi Rashid, man of miracles. Hear and answer the prayer offered to you at the Café Najma. Deliver us from their wickedness, corruption and their unions. Perform one of your miracles and replace evil with good, sinfulness with piety.

Suddenly there arose the sound of an oboe that seemed to fill the air with a sensuous yearning and desire. Shaykh Abdelmajid imagined it to be a sign of the coming of the Day of Judgement. He closed his eyes and muttered to himself: Forgive us our sins, O Lord, those we have committed and those we will commit. Let us die in the path of Your Prophet.

He thought about getting up and leaving this place and everyone in it. He remembered the mission which brought him here, in the heat of summer which only grew worse with every step he took, for nine gruelling hours. He calmed down.

This barber's shop must be the one that my brother-in-law Ammar owns. Let me go over and sit there for a while. That would be best. He'll most likely order me something cold to drink to put out the fire that's raging in my chest. If he doesn't, then I'll ask first.

'Are you coming from the capital, sir?'

'Yes, why do you ask?'

'Are you from the labour organization?'

'What labour organization?'

'The Music Arts Union? We're expecting a representative to come and organize local elections.'

'No,' replied Shaykh Boularwah, mumbling but emphatic. 'May God prevent you from any kind of union! May He make you all deaf. You've abandoned your responsibilities as sheep herders and sharecroppers, of harvesting alfalfa and prickly pears, all in order to learn the songs of the devils. You've assaulted the cities and corrupted men and women. You encourage immoral and licentious behaviour.'

'Would you like something to drink, uncle?' asked the waiter.

He snapped out of his gloomy trance and looked up.

'Yes, something cold. But please bring me a glass of water first. I'm dying of thirst.'

'Certainly.'

He gulped down the water in one mouthful and sat up straight in the chair. He felt a little more relaxed and started to look around him.

They act as though this arcade was built just for them. Three coffee shops right next to each other. Two barber's shops, a bathhouse. The old men look gaunter, more depressed than the young men whose facial expressions exude composure and self-confidence. Perhaps these old men feel as though they've been made outcasts in their own society and they look the way they do because they're ashamed. Whatever the case may be, whether they're outcasts or respected, they're definitely of a different temperament than these Soviet-looking young men.

This young man standing in front of me has the pretensions of a cultivated urbanite, a man of the world, and he affects the wisdom of a sage. God damn him, a bastard son-of-a-bitch! How can I possibly talk to such people intelligently? I think I'll start up a conversation with him to see from what side of him water flows, as they say.

'Hey there sonny, listen!'

'Are you talking to me?'

'Yes, you. Come here, please. I'd like to ask you something.'

'Gladly,' responded the young man, smiling.

He brought his chair close to Shaykh Boularwah, who had made a great effort to maintain his composure. Feigning a smile, he asked:

'Where are you from?'

'From Algeria.'

'Yes, I know from Algeria, but Algeria is made up of different people and tribes, like Arabs, Berbers, Turks, you know.'

'The Algerians are one people, uncle. We may not all have the same blood running through our veins, but we all live off the same soil.'

'Ah, very good! And what do you do for a living?'

'I'm an artist!'

'How wonderful. What kind of art do you practise?'

'Music. I'm a musician. I play the flute and the oboe.'

'Where did you learn how to play?'

'In my village.'

'Where is your village?'

Before he responded, the young man flashed a smile as though to say that he was no fool and that he was merely agreeing to satisfy the strange curiosity of an old man.

'I'm from the village of Ansar. Do you know where it is?'

'Yes, I know, it's close to Milia. What did you do before becoming a musician?'

'What would you expect me to do in Ansar or Milia? My father was a sharecropper who worked on land owned by a doctor who lived in the capital. He got to work on a few acres of land one year, then for the next five years had no work at all. I would do odd jobs from one summer to the next. I'd work two months or so, then sit idle for another ten months. What could I do, steal? Go to Europe? What could someone like myself possibly do besides learn songs and sing them? So a wedding celebration would bring me twenty thousand old francs in addition to the coin or two that would be thrown my way and which I'd have to share with the drummer and the dancer. Everyone makes do as best he can.'

'If I gave you a piece of land in Ansar or in Milia, would you accept it?'

'I, personally, would not. But my father, or my nine brothers who are all able to work, they'd accept a piece of land anywhere, be it Ansar, Ain Baida or even as far away as Oran. Are you from the government, sir?'

'Yes and no. I'm the director of a high school in Algiers.'

'Then how can you say you're not from the government? You are the government and it's a pleasure to meet you, sir. I went to the capital last year. They had written down on my papers that I was a soldier in the army, but I'm only in the reserves. So I went and had the error corrected.'

'Do you also have a record of military service?'

'Sure, why not? I'm proud to say that I'm in the reserves. The truth of the matter is that I am a soldier and I did complete my military training. I even participated in some major skirmishes. But since I didn't wear a military uniform and since I maintained contact with civilians from the cities and villages while on military missions, I was only given the title of "reservist" on my military record.'

'Why doesn't the government give you a job?'

'Do you think it can employ fourteen million Algerians? My oldest boy started high school this year. You see, I married young. I was only fifteen when I got married.'

Shaykh Abdelmajid Boularwah sat still for a moment and said nothing. He cracked his knuckles and swallowed his saliva. He wished to himself that this flute and oboe player would be struck by ruination and castration. He felt like telling him that had he or any of his brothers received one inch of his land, it would be as if they were pissing on his grave. But he restrained himself, especially since the young man announced that he would pay for the shaykh's drink, in deference to his being the director of a high school and to all high-school directors. Then he expressed his hope that his son would go to high school and receive a state scholarship, become an engineer or perhaps even a musicologist.

If the son of someone like yourself could advance so high, what would you expect of the son of a prosperous man, a physician or an engineer? Who would remain to prepare the wheat, churn the butter, gather the eggs and spin the wool? Just like that, all of a sudden, from the bottom of the pit, from the lowest of the low, to the highest of the high! My God, did you ever see such insolence? This government of evil has indeed opened your eyes!

Shaykh Boularwah wanted to say all of this to the young man, but he held back in consideration of the fact that the man was showing him respect by paying for his drink and that in the long run he really wasn't worth the bother. The young man waited for a response from the shaykh, but with none forthcoming, he flashed a smile to show his forgiveness of the shaykh for not having wished his son success and long life.

'If your school were in Constantine, my dear sir, I would certainly enrol my son in it.'

'No, no!' Shaykh Boularwah started to react at such an exaggerated display of politeness, but stopped suddenly as though he were sorry.

The taste of the drink is still in my mouth and there's something else I want to ask him.

'What I mean is that all the teachers in my school are from the East, from Egypt, Syria, Iraq, Lebanon and Tunisia. They miss classes frequently and they don't care much about the education of our children.'

'But, Professor.'

'Forget it. Let's get off the subject. Do you know the owner of that barber's shop over there?'

'Vaguely. I get my hair cut there every once in a while.'

'I'm looking for a barber named Ammar. He used to work here a long time ago.'

'This one's name is Ibrahim. He was already here when I first came.'

'Don't you know if there's any barber here at all in the arcade named Ammar?'

'Not that I know of. Go and ask the barber himself.'

'That's an idea!'

Shaykh Abdelmajid Boularwah got up slowly and worked his way through the tables and chairs, heading in the direction of the annoying sounds of oboe playing. He turned around and from the corner of his eye stole a glance at the barber who was standing outside. He stopped at the narrow entrance of the barber's shop.

One cuts hair while four wait their turn. They're taking up all the room in the shop. I'll ask him from here. He raised his voice:

'God have mercy on you and yours. Allow me to ask you a question.'

'Please go right ahead, my good man.'

'Do you know what happened to Ammar, the barber? He used to work here.'

'No sir, I don't. I've not heard of any barber by that name since I've come here.'

'When did you come?'

'I've been here the longest in the arcade, after Shaykh Nino the pawnbroker. It's been nine years since I came and the arcade is only ten years old.'

Nine years, that is, since the day after independence, or maybe since the eve of independence. He came on the heels of a Jew or a European who once owned the place. He probably used to cut hair in some back alley of the city on a crate, or maybe in a village somewhere. And in a blink of an eye, he finds himself in a barber's salon, equipped and fully furnished. And here he is thinking he's the first one in the arcade, the first maybe on the whole boulevard, or Constantine itself. No doubt he sees himself as one of the first city dwellers, here even before the Turks. Damn him and that cocky look he's directing at me.

'And where might this Nino be? The truth is, Ammar the barber was here even before the war.'

'Listen, uncle. Life is like running water. It's constantly changing course. This arcade has seen lots of changes since independence. First the magicians tried to occupy the place but they didn't last a week. Then the black marketeers tried to claim it but failed. The goldsmiths followed suit as did a group of cobblers, but they all ended up disappointed. Then there was a succession of artisans and craftsmen who all came and failed except for those you see here now. The arcade is not a very busy place, as you can see by these café chairs that block the way. The only people who pass by here are those who come for some specific reason. Actually, it's probably all for the better for those of us who are here.'

Do they think this place was built for them exclusively from the beginning?

Ibrahim, the barber, was rambling on about what he knew about the history of the arcade while Shaykh Boularwah, with his arm against the wall, kept his head bent down despondently as he listened.

Everything begins at point zero for these people. The world begins and ends with them. Maybe that's the history of the city from the first day. It ended with the Berbers and started with the Romans. It continued beginning and ending between Berbers and Romans and other peoples until the Arabs came. The city resumed its history with them until the Turks arrived. It went on like that until the French landed. And here we are now beginning and ending once again.

The earthquake which is going to be the demise of this whore of a city hasn't come yet. When it does, it will do so with a vengeance and will take revenge against its sordid past.

'O, Nino, Uncle Nino,' shouted Ibrahim the barber.

Shaykh Boularwah turned around and looked out at the street that ran along the arcade. There were some *jubba*-sellers sitting in rows of chairs against a wall next to a bookstall.

An old man was coming towards him. He was wearing a shabby black overcoat and a fez that was red on the top half and black and red on the bottom half. He had a wool burnous and a *jubba* draped over his arm. He was carrying a radio in his left hand and a delicate gold chain in his right which he was rolling through his fingers.

No doubt, this is Nino. I had forgotten him. Here he is, in the flesh, but how much his condition has deteriorated!

Nino was a businessman who trafficked in court cases. He would approach a litigant and, for a certain sum of money, assume all responsibilities in his suit against the opponent. He would hire the lawyer, oversee and help bring about a sentence, and even accompany the convicted to their executions. Whoever was approached by Nino with such an offer and refused was sure to lose his case. And you can be sure that whoever accepted always won, whatever the case. Look at him now, poor thing, auctioning his wares in the arcade, an old burnous, a tattered *jubba*, a small transistor and a thin gold chain. It must be nostalgia for this place that brings him back, nostalgia for the good old days, his old influential friends and his glories now since past.

'How are you, Nino? Are things still going well for you?'

'Who's that I see? Shaykh Boularwah? Will wonders never cease? Just recently someone was asking about you. But I don't remember who it was. How are you?'

The two men embraced and headed for a table that was about to be vacated.

'I've seen just about everybody from the old days except you. No one has seen or heard a word about you. How goes it with our Knower of Evil? I remember Shaykh Idir well, God have mercy on his soul. He used to say: "Most people benefit from my money, but Shaykh Boularwah gives it that extra vim and vigour whenever it falls into his hands." The last I heard, you were in Tunisia.'

Nino continued to ask questions while Shaykh Abdelmajid sat in quiet resignation. He replied:

'I'm fine, thanks be to God. And all of you here, how are you doing?'

'Do you remember . . .?' asked Nino.

'First, tell me, how did you get to be like this? What caused you to hit rock bottom?'

'I thank God, Shaykh Boularwah, for my long life and good eyesight. Thank God for that. Whatever has happened, I don't regret the past. We must all be content with our present and hope for the best for the future of our children. So why dwell on the past with regret? What's past is past. We made mistakes. We hurt other people and we hurt ourselves. But all things must pass. Thank God for long life and good eyesight, Shaykh Boularwah. Whoever thought that all of this would happen? I personally was one of those who firmly believed that the will of France was mightier than the will of God. It never occurred to me that the iron will of France would bend one day, that France would be humiliated and defeated, leaving us Algeria.'

'Leaving them Algeria.'

'No, us, all of us, Shaykh Boularwah, even me. Yes, even me.'

His eyes watered, his jaw dropped and his lips quivered as he spoke. He continued, mumbling:

'At the time, my oldest son was in jail, and my youngest was up in the mountains, and I . . .'

He was unable to finish his sentence. Tears rolled from his eyes and there was a lump in his throat. He bowed his head in shame.

'Did you collaborate with the French secret police?' asked Shaykh Abdelmajid.

Nino motioned with his head that he had. After a moment he continued to speak:

'May God forgive me, if not . . .'

Shaykh Abdelmajid Boularwah wondered to himself why most traitors seem resigned to their fate. Is it out of some kind of self-flattery, or is it that they feel tolerant having been granted tolerance?

If France had won the war, what would have been the fate of Nino? An agha, pashagha, or leader of some kind, no doubt! But what about his two sons in the Resistance? The soldier son would have been martyred along with those who were with him. The imprisoned son would have been released through his father's intercession and forced to abandon his principles.

Nino's future was shattered, or the way he sees it, the future of France, Europe and all of Africa.

A grand colonialist future has been destroyed ...

But what on earth has taken its place?

God forgive me, independence is independence and victory is victory. Socialism and communism are something else. God will appoint for His religion men who will reclaim its power and majesty, not only in Algeria but all over the Muslim world. But in all these liberated countries, like Morocco, Tunisia, Syria or Egypt, you see the signs of heresy and freethinking. Had France remained here, especially after the war we waged against her, she would have forced all of us to abandon our faith and embrace Christianity. Now, if the elite of this country, both the wealthy and the clerics, stand united, on guard against the designs of these freethinkers, and keep them from achieving their goals, then this nation will be saved and our religion will remain intact.

Nino sat with his head bowed down, staring into space ...

'Even though he was heavily disguised, I recognized him. I followed him from here, to Souiqa and then to Jabiya Gate. He went into the third room of the brothel. Na'naa closed the door behind him. It was midday. The city was covered in snow. What should I do? Should I go back and call my commander, or stay and wait to find out where his hiding place was? There was no problem for me personally to stay at the brothel other than the possibility of being exposed to a scandal by one of my acquaintances. But if my back was turned plotting with my commander he could easily escape. I approached the door and pretended to tie my shoes and adjust the laces.

"Na'naa, did you do everything I told you to do?"

"Yes, everything is fine!"

"I want you to go out right away!"

"As you like."

"Here's ten thousand francs. Take it to my wife and have her take my son to the doctor and pay the fees. Here's a list of the medicine that I want you to buy for us."

"And you?"

"I'll wait for him to come out first. When you come back, we'll try to leave together."

'I ran to the post office and called the commander to inform him of what was happening. Then I went back to the brothel and waited by the entrance, as he instructed.

'Military jeeps and civilian cars were moving in all directions. Constantine was surrounded. The gates and passageways at Sidi Rashid were blocked off. They stationed a battalion at the bottom of the Jabiya Gate road, and another at the entrance to the main gate. The commander approached. He pounded on the door with all his might while the soldiers raised their rifles.

"Ammar, we know you're in there. There's a blockade all around the city. Sidi Rashid is blocked off, so is the Jabiya Gate. We even have the room you're in blockaded. There's no use resisting. Give yourself up or we'll smoke you out with tear gas. It's all over, Ammar!"

'While the commander was shouting his orders, the army arrested everyone in the brothel, men and women alike, and took them to the military trucks. Then they arrested me so that no one would suspect what I was doing there.

"Bring me the old man who's acting like a child so that I can see for myself what he's up to. I have no doubt it was Ammar who brought him here. Why else would he be here?"

'Ammar did not come out.

"I'm giving you one last chance. It's all over, there's no way to escape. Come out now or we'll storm the room. I'll count to three, then I'll do whatever it takes to force you out!"

'Ammar did not come out.

"One . . ."

'Ammar did not come out.

"Two . . ."

'Ammar did not come out.'

"Two . . .", repeated the commander, seething with anger.

"I'm coming out," shouted a voice from inside. "I'm coming out and giving myself up."

'That voice, I knew it, but whose could it be? I wondered. My heart was beating violently, that voice was ringing familiar in my ear. But whose could it be?

"That's better. Now, throw your weapons down on the ground first."

"I'm opening the door. I'll throw out my machine gun, then I'm coming out!"

"No, no, Slaiman, my son! What a horror! My God!"

'I was struck in the mouth with the butt of a rifle. There was blood. My eyes practically popped out of their sockets. The door opened and there immediately followed the explosion of a grenade, then another. People began to scream and smoke filled the air. Bodies dropped to the ground and you could hear the rapid pounding of footsteps. Since no one was holding me, I sneaked to the rear. Then the sound of gunfire erupted. I stared at the door of the room, then looked up and down the street. More grenades exploded. A voice I knew only too well cried out: "My dear mother".

'Some time soon after it all died down, I was brought to the entrance of Na'naa's room to identify the body. There were two, Ammar's body and the body of my son, Slaiman.

'May God have mercy on the martyrs,' muttered Nino, as he looked at Shaykh Abdelmajid Boularwah, who abruptly cut him off to ask him a question:

'I want to ask you about a barber who used to work here. His name is Ammar. I'm sure you know him.'

'May God have mercy on the martyrs,' answered Nino, as he sighed in grief.

Nino explained that it was this Ammar who had died a martyr-hero's death and who left behind a son who would now be sixteen years old. Shaykh Abdelmajid Boularwah got up and left the arcade on the main boulevard.

My brother-in-law a martyr, what an honour! My wife will be delighted when she hears of this. I won't contact his son though. It would probably end up costing me money.

He was inundated by the waves of odours coming at him from all directions: grilled sweetbreads, sauces, spices, prickly pears. Waves of people were crashing against him. The noise was getting louder, to the point of being frightening. Car horns were crying out for help. People were screaming at each other, repeating sentence after sentence as though they were all deaf.

The dark shadow was moving inside him. That viscous fluid was melting. It was getting hotter. He was growing weak in the knees. His neck was getting stiff and his head was pounding. He felt an enormous weight on his shoulders. Two men walking in front of him were blocking his way, but he was able to overhear their conversation.

'They're all fighting one another over sugar. Somebody buys forty pounds and he's still looking for more.'

'That's the way life is sometimes, Tahir Ben Ali. They hoard whenever Ramadan approaches. There's not a drop of oil to be found in any of the stores.'

'There's no flour or soap. Every home has turned into a store-house.'

'Life is like that, Tahir Ben Ali.'

Shaykh Abdelmajid leaned over as he eavesdropped on the conversation between the two men who were blocking his way. Then he thought to himself: it's not enough this weight they put upon this poor, miserable rock, but they have to go and hoard massive amounts of food as well . . .

You could say, then, that the weight has doubled . . .

It'll be fast. No sooner will the rock tremble than everything will come tumbling down, falling apart. The ravines will split wide open and swallow up everybody, along with all the oil, sugar and semolina. And then they will close up again. Everything will become flat.

During all of this there will be great panic! 'Every suckling female will forget her suckling, and every pregnant female will discharge her burden, and you will see men drunk, yet it will not be in intoxication.' No, no. More likely, every hoarder of oil, sugar and semolina will abandon what he's hoarded. Everyone carrying a basket or a shopping bag will drop it and everyone will stop talking for a moment. This is the description of the Earthquake of Doom for Constantine. The suckling female will forget her suckling only after she runs through the streets chasing after food. All the foetuses in the stomachs of these heathen bitches mean less than five gallons of oil, or five pounds of sugar. And could all these men possibly be more drunk than they are now? They've been showing signs of drunkenness for a long time.

He was finally able to cross the narrow street. He stood there as people coming from every direction pushed him with their hands, shoulders and even their stomachs. He was pushed so far back that he was pinned up against the wall.

Whom shall I ask about first? Tahir the pickpocket at Camels' Square or Issa the Sufi mystic at the shrine of Sidi Abdelmu'min? I should start at Camels' Square then swing over to the shrine, and then go down to pray at the mausoleum of Sidi Rashid.

Shaykh Abdelmajid Boularwah mumbled to himself as he started to make his way slowly up the hill from which he would turn off towards the main square.

At one end you can hear Ferghani singing and at the other Umm Kulsoum.[1] Across the way you can hear a religious sermon on the radio. Close by is the voice of Issa Jarmouni and a few steps away Farid al-Atrash. In the midst of it all is the sound of: *This is London*. And a cacophony of odours fills the air.

Plastic on your ID card, plastic on your driver's licence! Get plastic, fast and easy, and all for a low price!

---

1. Famous Egyptian singer, popular throughout the Arab world (d. 1975).

The last phrase, '*and all for a low price*', caught his attention. He turned around. There stood a young man of seventeen in a shabby blue Mao suit wearing straw sandals. He had long hair and a pasty complexion with red blotches on his face. He held his nose in the air and his full lips were ready to crack a self-assured smile at any moment. His eyes were intense and his hand movements steady and composed. He was sitting at a small table on top of which were a red press, some rolls of paper and a blank identity card.

Young people are so calm and collected these days, it makes me nervous! They're so self-contained and self-assured. They act as though they've cut themselves totally free from all the grown-ups. Every young man in this city appears to be neither happy nor sad. They all go to such trouble to free their lives of any complications. You'd think their lives began in reverse, from old to young.

'A watch. A watch.'

'A transistor. A transistor.'

'A tape recorder . . .'

'A pair of shoes . . .'

'A briefcase . . .'

'A pair of trousers . . .'

'An overcoat . . .'

'A watch . . .'

'A brand-new transistor.'

'A brand-new camera.'

Hands are outstretched, tongues wagging, bodies rock back and forth, but the feet are not moving.

At first Shaykh Abdelmajid Boularwah responded by saying 'no' to everything that was pushed in his face. But gradually he conveyed his refusal with an expression of silent disdain as he looked absent-mindedly at the merchandise.

I'm absolutely certain that every Constantinian is either a thief or a victim of theft. People pass the time robbing one another, then selling what they've stolen back to each other. Their merchandise, like their money, spends the night in one place and wakes up in the morning in another. It grows on what comes from outside the country and diminishes by being squandered in the countryside! These people are doing nothing here, just coming and going in one long, continuous circle, displaying their goods to each other. Even though it's summertime and people walk around barefoot, you see a cobbler every few steps hammering and stitching like there's no tomorrow. These people have nothing to do but walk around, with no job or skill to hold them in one place. Maybe this is why they all left their small towns and villages.

The thought made him stop and think.

Unemployment is the reason why all these people hang about in Constantine so shamelessly. It's like this in all the agricultural areas. One hand produces and a thousand mouths consume. One man breaks his back while a thousand others sit and watch. They work sixty days a year and sit idle three hundred.

The people who dreamed up this diabolic scheme must have been thinking about all this: Let's usurp the lands of pious, God-fearing people and distribute them to the masses! Just so one person can have a few square feet of land, or maybe one or two chickens. Then the cities would be evacuated, or at least, the population explosion would slow down.

That was the idea!

These damned heathens! The Russians brainwashed them with their insane ideas and they applied them to the letter, but all too slowly. This logic they're using is totally wrong and their way of thinking is much too simplistic.

Who's going to leave the city and who's going to remain? Those gullible enough to bite the bait of fast talk and empty promises are like flies! Their women got used to having their bathhouses and hospitals while their kids flock to the schools and playgrounds. They'll never leave the city. The ones who stay behind in the small towns and villages have nothing but the garbage dumps to look forward to and swarm over like flies.

What a thought!

Instead of the government winning these people over to its side, the people revolt against the government. They have to be convinced that their connection is to the land. It's a modern idea whose message should be to stop these people from migrating to the cities. The fact of the matter is that this was the original idea. All of these government people themselves left the countryside and came to the cities where they put down their roots until the time came to face the problem of overcrowding and congestion. The government doesn't like to beat around the bush. It knows too well that a situation like this is a natural result. It's not simply a show by the masses, protesting and demanding that the borders to Europe and America be opened.

Shaykh Abdelmajid felt some sort of relief after he passed the outstretched hands, the loud voices, and all those bodies bumping into one another. He turned towards the owners of the small shops and muttered to himself:

Camels' Square is just as it's always been. Yet it's so narrow, it couldn't hold fifty camels! Whatever possessed its settlers to give it such a name? It must have been wider then and slowly it got smaller. Every time a camel left it, its owner would settle down in its place.

He headed towards the closest café and plopped down on the first chair he bumped into. He looked all around, inside and out. The metal tables and chairs were freshly painted, as were the walls. An Italian espresso machine had replaced the old cooking range.

Even here!

Besides the owner, I'm the only one sitting here. Naturally, everyone else is out walking or getting their shoes repaired.

The owner of the café, middle-aged and well over fifty, seems to be in good shape. He's tall and fair-skinned. His turban is neat and tightly wrapped around his head, a sign of a Constantinian of good stock. His features are those of a refined and dignified man, giving him a statuesque quality.

I'm sure he knows Tahir, the pickpocket, or at least what's become of him. He's watching me from the corner of his eye, not moving a muscle. Even if he used to know me, he most certainly must have

forgotten me after all this time. In fact, I rarely came to Camels'
Square. When he comes over, I'll ask him. But will I have to order
something to drink? I don't have a lot of time and I really can't afford
to waste what little I have of it. I've got to leave Constantine tonight
and spend the night in the village. I need to settle accounts with the
tenant farmers before kicking them off the land. From now on, I'll
only work my lands with machines and seasonal workers. Who knows
with these bandits! Let me get up and ask him, then I'll leave.

'Excuse me, may I ask you something?'

'Certainly! Go right ahead!'

'I'm looking for a relative of mine who used to be here a long time
ago. I've lost contact with him. His name is Tahir.'

'Half the population of Constantine is named Tahir! Where was
his shop?'

'He didn't own a shop. He did odd jobs, here and there. His family
name is Boularwah, like mine. Tahir Boularwah.'

'Oh, yes. Why didn't you say so at the beginning. Si Tahir!'

'Si Tahir?'

'Haven't you heard? You must be coming from abroad.'

'I'm his uncle. I was in Tunisia for many years during the war.
Since independence I've been in Algiers. The truth is, because of his
past, as you know, we were cut off from one another.'

'What past are you talking about, sir? Si Tahir was one of our
leading nationalists. He was thrown in jail more than once, condemned for a bunch of trumped-up charges. They used to say he was
a pickpocket. But in fact, he used to smuggle weapons and
ammunition. Tahir was one of the leaders!'

'I'm his uncle. Where is he now?'

'I'm his father-in-law. He married my daughter after he came back
from the mountains. He divorced his first wife and became my son-in-
law.'

'We're in-laws, then?'

'I guess so! Please have something to drink.'

'With pleasure.'

Accepting the invitation, Shaykh Abdelmajid Boularwah sat down as his host went off to get him a drink. He wondered whether he should first ask him his opinion about the government or ask about the fate of his nephew whose name was now attached to the honorific title of 'Si'. If, in fact, this fellow really is an independent merchant, then surely he must despise the government. I've never met a merchant who didn't hate the government. Real merchants are natural capitalists and well respected, not swindlers like Belbey and Nino. If it turns out he does hate the government, then I let him in on my secret, so that he'll know that those whom this matter concerns should band together to stop this project. Whether he hates the government or not, I must talk to him a little bit about this diabolic scheme. He could then alert all those who would be affected by it, in one way or another, so that everyone, whether involved or not, will revolt against it.

'Please do me the honour of having dinner at my home this evening. It's the least I can do.'

'May God increase your prosperity! But I was hoping to leave the city tonight.'

'I wouldn't hear of it. The uncle of my son-in-law comes to town and leaves without breaking bread with me?'

'Allow me to present myself. I am Abdelmajid Boularwah, the uncle of your son-in-law Tahir. I'm the director of a high school in Algiers. I'm a scholar of religion and classical Arabic. Haven't you ever heard of me?'

'Si Tahir spoke to us of you. Yes, he spoke of you.'

The café owner spoke and then stopped to think to himself: 'A good workhorse doesn't get sold!' All this time he never came to ask about him, and then all of a sudden he shows up and introduces himself as his uncle.

'To tell you the truth, he never spoke to me about his work or his plans. They used to say that he was a pickpocket at Camels' Square.'

'These were accusations that the colonialist authorities made against him.'

'It pained me, in fact, it infuriated me the day he decided to sell his land. Can you imagine? I had to go into debt to be able to buy it so that it would stay in the family.'

'He did talk about selling his land. He said he was forced to so that he wouldn't lose an important shipment of arms.'

'If only he'd asked us then, we would have given him anything. After all, he is my nephew and this was our national cause.'

'I saw him pull a dagger on his fellow pickpockets with my own eyes. Then I heard the details of his trial and how he confessed to stealing the wallet of an old Jewish woman which had four hundred old francs in it.'

Everything begins with them! There's no one like them when you're creating history.

Whatever the case may be, the honour of the nephew reflects well on the uncle and vice versa. Who knows, maybe he's a big merchant or the owner of a factory or something along those lines. He may even have sons to whom I could sign over some of my property. I'll kill twenty birds with one stone. I won't dwell on the past. I'll live for the present and strengthen my ties to my relatives. That way, I'll make sure that the government doesn't get its hands on my property. That's what's important! I'll make sure that the vast bulk of my land remains within the family in the event of my death. He's my sole beneficiary, that is, according to Islamic law. But who knows, with these infidels running the government!

'My name is Sa'dan Belarabi. I've been here at this café for thirty years. I first met Si Tahir when he was very young. He used to sit over there in that corner with his head up and his eyes wandering in every direction. Before we found out what he really did, we used to think he was a police informer. We even thought about having him assassinated.'

'Weren't you at all afraid of the police? Surely you yourself were part of the movement?'

Sa'dan thought of responding immediately by saying that he had been in the movement, but for some inexplicable reason, he hesitated.

Then he bit his lower lip, shut his eyes and then opened them wide.

'We were supposed to bring in shipments of soap at any cost. Two hundred shipments weighing about two tons to be paid for in advance. We all pooled together whatever money we could scrape up. I sold all my furniture. I even took out a mortgage on the café. In fact, I sold most of my shares in it to cover the costs. It was a matter of life and death for each and every one of us. Fifty donkeys were to bring in fifty shipments through Batua and Ain Mlila and wait at Bardo. Fifty others were to come in through Ain Baida and Ain Kirsha and wait at Sidi Mabrouk. The third fifty would come in through Guelma and Wadi Zenati and wait at Jabal Wahsh. The last fifty would pass through Azzaba and wait at Hama.

'The shipment was sold to us in Tunisia. I travelled to Tebessa to sign the contract and put the final touches on the deal. It was up to me to safeguard this huge shipment and save my own neck at the same time. I had to keep all this a secret and stay clear of the French spies and their German agents. At this time Tahir started to come around the square and hang out at the café. One day, I left him here, and later when I got to Ain Baida, I went into a bathhouse to spend the night. There he was, right before my very eyes. I tried to avoid him, but he recognized me. He was just a kid but sharp as a pistol. He stared at me as though wondering what I was doing there. Was I following him or chasing him away? Then he closed his eyes and fell asleep. The next morning when I awoke, he was gone. We knew him at the square as Qadour, but when I asked the bath attendant about him, he told me his name was Boujum'a and that he came from Setif. He wasn't an informant at all, I thought, but a smuggler.

'I continued on my journey. When I got to Tebessa, sure enough there he was. We both pretended not to notice one another until we ended up next to each other at a bathhouse. He still hadn't been known as a pickpocket then, but I was cautious just the same. I didn't sleep and I kept one hand on my dagger and the other on the sack of money that was tied around my waist. Thank God, the sale took place quickly. I didn't waste any time loafing about in Tebessa. The first precaution I took was to propose to my colleagues that we get rid of him. The problem is that he disappeared only to resurface four and a half years later. We later found out that he had joined up with the German forces and then was taken prisoner and forced into the French army.

'Our donkey convoys fell into an ambush of guard patrols, but most of us escaped unharmed. We bribed our way through a slew of captains, secret agents and forest guards until we safely accomplished our mission. A few days later, Constantine was up to its ears in soap.'

Deep in thought about the remote past, Sa'dan was recalling many of its details, while Abdelmajid Boularwah himself gave way to his own thoughts provoked by the mention of the police.

'The day one of our senior colleagues was arrested, I did everything in my power to let the informers know who we really were. I went to all the cafés and talked to as many people as I could. I let the word out that we were strictly a religious organization with no political affiliations or aspirations. I let it be known that we shared the authorities' view on the separation of state and religion but that we only asked for freedom to conduct our business.

'At the Café Najma I gave my word that I would not correspond with arrested colleagues, not one message. I even swore to divorce my wife if there was ever any contact between myself and anyone in prison. I kept my word and, as far as I know, so did the others. That's what led him to compose a poem implicating us. The police are evil. The unions are evil. Violence is evil.'

'A Swiss watch, twenty-four carat gold!'

'Radio cassette recorder, from Tindouf!'

'Custom-made suits from Shanghai!'

The sounds grew louder as waves of vendors suddenly descended onto the café while the sirens of police cars screeched in every direction. In no time the café was so full of people, some standing, some seated, that you hardly had room to breathe.

The Earthquake of Doom is a horrendous thing. The day it strikes 'every suckling female will forget her suckling, and every pregnant female will discharge her burden, and you will see men drunk, yet it will not be in intoxication . . .' La Brèche Square must have opened its mouth wide and those who hadn't been swallowed up fled here. After a while, the west side will melt away and people will seek refuge in the east side. Then it will tip over and everything will fall to pieces. Rocks will come tumbling down on top of one another and you will see flesh and bones, oil and sugar, soap and semolina spilling out and splashing in every direction. Gas tanks will explode and electric wires will release a shower of sparks. The flames of the fire, mixed with dust and smoke, will shoot up into the sky. Thus the wicked, sinful city will come to an end and the only thing left for the people to do will be to steal from each other and fornicate.

And me?

Condemned, with all my enemies, O Lord. No, I beseech you. I want to bear witness to the end of these wicked traitors and the failure of their evil schemes. I want to see the word of God rule over all the world; I want His word to be the only thing that remains forever and always.

The crowd grew thicker. Vendors, thieves, hawkers and passers-by gathered around the café and the adjacent shops. Some of them had crawled under the wall that stood on one side of the café while others had jumped over it.

'Sebti, Sebti!' cried out Sa'dan.

A young man looked in his direction. He had wrist-watches wrapped around the fingers of his left hand, and with his right hand he was holding a radio and a pair of shoes. With both his shoulders, Sebti pushed his way through the crowd who were blocking his way, people of all ages and sizes, until he reached Sa'dan.

'Good evening, Uncle Sa'dan. How's it going?'

'What happened?'

'Murjana is dead.'

'And who's this Murjana?'

'A new girl who works out of Bab al-Jabiya. Her pimp came with her from Jelfa. The other pimps tried to take her away but the Jelfa pimp defended her to the death. They stabbed him and he stumbled towards the ground, but he managed to turn towards her and stab her several times before he died. All the other pimps fled, but now the police have Sidi Rashid surrounded. They're asking to see the identity card of everyone who leaves. Anyone who doesn't have one will be interrogated and searched. Apparently, they're going to stay until things calm down. Poor Murjana was only sixteen years old, fair-skinned, tall and slender, with a kind heart. God have mercy on her soul!'

The siege of the quarter by the police didn't last very long and Abdelmajid left Sa'dan's café soon thereafter. He was lost in thought as he continued on his way.

Here is a bathhouse with a broken wooden board nailed across the door. In horrible handwriting painted in red the sign reads: *Today, women only*! What self-respecting woman would dare to set foot in this square, much less patronize this sleazy bathhouse? . . . But then again, if there weren't any female customers, why would the proprietor bother to hang up such a sign?

People around here don't take much notice of one another. Everybody does exactly what he wants, as though he were all alone, with no one to watch him or stand in his way. They all stick out their hands at one another, everybody trying to sell something. No one seems to agree with anyone else, nor for that matter do they disagree. They don't feel each other's presence, but at the same time, they can't seem to do without one another. If this isn't the hour of the earthquake, then I don't know what is. I wonder when it will come.

Then Shaykh Abdelmajid thought about the last thing Sa'dan said.

'Tahir is a high-ranking officer. Haven't you heard? He's powerful and influential.'

'What rank is he?'

'Come closer, so that I can whisper in your ear.'

'Could he have changed his name?'

'That's exactly what he did.'

'Tonight, we'll have dinner at my place. First, we'll perform the sunset prayers at the Grand Mosque, then we'll head home.'

'Don't trouble yourself.'

'The matter is settled, Shaykh Abdelmajid. We're in-laws.'

Tahir Boularwah, the pickpocket, my drunken, trouble-making nephew, a high-ranking officer? And not just any officer! Powerful and influential! Now this presents a problem. The earthquake is a sensation you feel, before it comes, after and during. Belbey, Nino and Sa'dan have all felt it coming. But me?

I'm waiting, waiting for it to come . . .

'Every suckling female will forget her suckling, and every pregnant female will discharge her burden, and you will see men drunk, yet it will not be in intoxication.' The people will forget all about sugar, coffee, soap and semolina, about buying and selling, and stealing from one another. Rocks will come crashing down, and there will be huge cracks in the earth. Fires will ignite everywhere, then all will be subdued. 'We are certainly able to bring better people than they in their place, and they will not be able to thwart us.'

That thing is growing heavier in my chest and that rotting smell is getting stronger. The viscous liquid is running through my veins and I've got this bitter taste in my mouth. The obnoxious odour of the peel of prickly pears, the smells of the cobbler shops and the stench of urine are inescapable.

As he turned to leave Camels' Square, Shaykh Abdelmajid walked into a long line of people, unbathed, barefoot and dressed in rags, carrying tin cans and utensils tied together with string and scraps of dirty cloth. On the wall where they were standing was a sign that read: *Municipal Soup Kitchen*! Ah, they're even feeding them. They insist that they need these people. Of course, naturally. Now they're all showing their true colours!

What's this country coming to? Tahir the pickpocket is a powerful and influential high-ranking officer. Ammar the barber is a martyr. Nino the auctioneer and traitor has a prominent son. Belbey is bankrupt and content with his lot in life. Sa'dan, soap and drug smuggler, is the father-in-law of a powerful and influential high-ranking officer.

O Prophet of God, Companion of God, you have spoken the truth. All the signs of the hour of doom have come. The barefoot, the downtrodden and the sheep herders construct high monuments and the servant gives birth to her mistress. Everything has been turned upside down and we don't know what's up and what's down. These are indeed the signs that the time has come. The Earthquake of Doom is indeed a horrendous thing.

He continued to mull over these thoughts in his mind as he staggered through an alley reeking with odours. With every step he stole a glance at the restaurants and shops around him. He was astonished by all the business that was going on inside them.

This little market-place hasn't changed a bit, except that there are a lot more people. The barber is reading a newspaper, but nobody is getting a haircut. The odours have started to lose their distinctiveness as everything blends together. Here the alleys are narrower. On the right, there's the Aragon School. In the old days anybody who wasn't educated at the Aragon School was considered illiterate by the educated elite, who sent their children only to French schools. Look how things have changed since then!

From above you can see Sidi Bou 'Anaba. Down below, one level down, is the shrine of Sidi Abdelmu'min. One level below that you reach the river and its banks, then the bridge and then the mausoleum of Sidi Rashid.

When I get to the shrine of Sidi Abdelmu'min, I'll ask about my nephew Issa. After that I'll pass by Sidi Rashid for the afternoon prayer. I'm sure Issa will still be there, reciting and teaching the Qur'an, writing out amulets and receiving visitors. He was always a model of mysticism, piety and probity. He learned by heart the *Ajurrumiyya* and the *Risala*. I'm certain that he studied Sidi Khalil[1]

---

1. Khalil b. Ahmad, early Arab grammarian and lexicographer and inventor of the Arabic system of metres (d. 791).

after that. He is a devout mystic and, of all the men I know, the man most removed from the world and its preoccupations. Events must have certainly taken place without his noticing and left him unscathed by all the horrible changes that have afflicted the people of this wicked city.

Even the walls of the city are leaning over backwards. When the earthquake comes, they will fall down and crash into the Rhumel Valley. Because the side streets are so narrow, you can hardly see the windows, yet you can see at every window a woman sitting and looking out. Satan's cows, they'd all be better off in caves and grottoes. There are so many children here. They're like locusts, devouring everything in their path through the city on their way to the top of the hill, dropping their eggs to hatch behind them.

O you bad seeds, procreators of evil! May God destroy you with a plague and send down an earthquake onto Constantine with you all in it, and may the Rhumel Valley gobble you up! Just look at all these young men sitting in the doorways, looking out, staring at nothing. Look how pathetic they are. Their lives mean nothing to them and they're not fazed in the least about dying. They've already died a thousand and one deaths! Suppose one of them grabs the controls of an aeroplane, you know what he'd do. Or if he grabs hold of someone's neck, he would slash it with a razor, without even blinking an eye. They're all so cocky and arrogant.

All the buildings are freshly painted, but then again, 'You can't judge a book by its cover!' Ah look, the shrine of Sidi Abdelmu'min, it's the one that's still painted green. Some things stay the same. Maybe the world isn't so bad after all, and the heart of the believer can take comfort that there may still be some hope left in this life that God will save us from the earthquake, and that He will prolong the life of the world and assure His pious servants an honourable means of living. Perhaps He will save us from the evil deeds of the wicked, godless traitors.

My nephew Issa will jump for joy when he sees me. He'll remember to remind me that his mother died in my house and that I gave her a respectable funeral. On that occasion people brought me sheep to be slaughtered, and lots of sugar and oil. I'll tell him that I've missed him and that I've gone to much trouble to find and visit him. I'll tell him that I've decided to give him back his lands provided that he take control of them after I die. On second thoughts, I won't have to make any conditions. It won't matter to him whether I put my land in his name or mine. What the world needs now is more people like him, holy and pious, free of the greed for material goods.

'Peace be upon you,' called out Shaykh Abdelmajid Boularwah as soon as he set foot in the doorway of the shrine.

A middle-aged man with a dour look on his face turned towards him and gave him a long, hard stare. Then he feigned a smile and beckoned him to come closer and take a seat close to the mihrab of the small mosque.

'Please come in and sit down.'

Even here things seem to have changed. But since there's someone here to greet visitors to the shrine, then matters can't be all that bad.

Shaykh Abdelmajid coughed to clear his throat, then raised his voice as he offered a limp hand to greet the caretaker of the shrine. The caretaker stared at the outstretched hand, amazed at his visitor's irreverence. Abdelmajid should have kissed his hand or clasped his shoulders or done nothing at all until he was asked.

'Thank you. I will sit down. I've come to inquire about a relative of mine. He used to be a caretaker at this shrine. That was a long time ago. The last time I saw him here was at the beginning of the war. I went to Tunisia, and as I got older I became more and more involved in my work in the capital. I was never able to get away to visit him until today. But I can't find him. You actually resemble him, but you're a lot older than he.'

'Perhaps you're asking about Sidi Boularwah?'

'Yes, Issa Boularwah. He's my nephew.'

'You've come too late, sir.'

'What are you saying? I hope nothing bad has happened to him!'

'Many strange things happened to him in his life that distressed him greatly.'

'How so?'

'He got involved first with the unions and then with the communists. That's between you and me.'

'Issa, the pious Sufi, becoming a unionist and a communist!'

'One day a man came to see him. His right arm was missing and he was wearing a blue suit. He sat down next to him saying:

"Sidi Boularwah, what am I going to do? I lost my arm while I was working for Machat's Company. I'm supposed to get workers' compensation since it happened on the job. But you know, Sidi, that Machat has close ties to all the authorities. Every time we try to start a new union, they come in and appoint one of their own to lead it. Machat's expensive gifts always find their way into the houses of high officials. This guy is like a little statue, a replica of the dearly departed France, which they all worship here in Constantine. They have forgotten all that we struggled for, we who survived and those who have died. They only recognize Machat's generosity and the fact that he never took a position against the revolution.

"You, Sidi, as God is my witness, you've known our holy struggle. You took to the hills and launched your resistance. But do any of the local officials remember you? Their idol is Machat, he alone! They came to the conclusion that I lost my arm during off-hours. They said I was intending to commit a robbery. They even tried and convicted me, but in the end, Machat forgave me and even decided not to make me pay him compensation for the machine which broke down for six days because of my injury.

"Sidi, what do you advise me to do? What do you think I should do? I have seven kids, a wife and a mother to feed. What is your answer to all of this, Sidi Boularwah?"

"File an appeal," responded Sidi Boularwah.

'The worker with the severed arm responded quickly:

"But, Sidi, you need a lawyer and you go through a lot of trouble gathering witnesses and making the right contacts with the union!"

"File an appeal and I'll take care of the costs," replied Sidi Boular-wah.

"The worker embraced Sidi Boularwah with his one arm as tears rolled down his cheeks."

'But that doesn't prove that Issa actually became a unionist!'

'Hold on. The matter doesn't end there. A week later, three men came by to see him. They said to him:

"Sidi Boularwah, we didn't come here to seek your blessings or to make an offering. That we can do another time, God willing. We are workers in a private company but a very big one. We held a meeting and invited everyone to attend. We voted to start a local chapter of the union, and that was all! The very next day the authorities issued a decree dissolving our local chapter. The decree was issued in the morning, and that evening, the leadership of the union fired all the workers who organized the meeting. That's the three of us.

"We didn't know what to do. The workers held a strike for two hours, but the authorities came in and broke it up. The result was more victims! We contacted the local authorities, but they wouldn't see us. They accused us of sabotage and of being agents for foreign communists. We've never been out of Constantine in our whole lives, Sidi, nor have we ever received so much as a letter from outside Algeria. We never even thought about anything outside the country. We wouldn't even know what to do with these foreign agents with whom we're supposed to have had ties. We're just union men and this is the first time we ever held elections!"

"Mobilize yourselves and all your co-workers!"

"But Sidi, what about the police? You know how tense people are right now!"

"Make contacts in Algiers. Go there yourselves. Some of you go while the rest stay here and try to recruit the workers!"

"We'll try, Sidi!"

"If it becomes a question of writing up a petition, then I'll do it. If it's a question of money, I'll give you whatever you need."

"How can we ever thank you, Sidi? The truth is, we'll need money just to get to Algiers!"

'Why did these scoundrels come to poor Issa in the first place?'

'He was the shaykh, their spiritual leader. He was the caretaker of the mosque where they'd been praying since they were born.'

'Whatever the case may be, this doesn't prove that Issa himself became a unionist.'

'Hold on! A week later Sidi Boularwah came to see me and told me this story about a certain Abu Dharr al-Ghaffari who appeared to him three times in a dream. I have no idea who this character is, but this is what he told me:

"Three times this man appeared to me in a dream. He said to me that the way to God was through serving His servants and through repelling those who resist Him. The way to God was to fight injustice and exploitation!"

'He performed his ablutions, prayed and then left the mosque. A few hours later, the police showed up and started asking me questions about him. Since that day he's gone underground, but he organizes strikes and distributes pamphlets. We hear that he's also in contact with student groups and workers. I'm convinced that the bug of unionism bit him long before the armed struggle for independence began. There's no security, even on safe ground!'

God damn him in the dark of night and the light of day, murmured Shaykh Abdelmajid Boularwah. As he walked along, he felt the earth tremble beneath his feet and the walls shake all around him. His eyes were growing heavier and heavier and that thick liquid was oozing up towards his brain, getting thicker and thicker all along the way. He put his hands on his forehead, covered his eyes and yelled out:

'The Earthquake of Doom is a horrendous thing. On that day every suckling female will forget her suckling. I implore you, Sidi Rashid, rid this city of all of them, their godlessness and iniquity.'

Shaykh Abdelmajid Boularwah left the shrine of Sidi Abdelmu'min and headed down towards Ahmed Hilal Street. He walked in a slow, deliberate manner, swaying from left to right. All of a sudden, he found himself in front of a house whose walls and windows leaned against another house, leaving just a tiny passage between the two houses for people to walk through. He stopped, then wiped his forehead with his fingers, leaned forward and resumed walking, taking wider steps. Then he came across a large, open space.

There are ruins over on the right. Once there were many houses on this spot, multi-storeyed, where people used to breathe easy, eat and drink, sleep and wake, love and hate, suffer pain and commit licentious acts. One night they went to sleep and never woke up! A rock beneath them shook and the walls of their houses came tumbling down on top of them.

Maybe they went out one morning to do their errands, to sell their contraband, have their shoes patched or to buy some prickly pears. And when they came home they found nothing but piles of earth heaped upon the corpses of their wives and children. Whatever the case may be, they were spared the dreadful anticipation of the earthquake, that constant feeling of anxiety and confusion.

He continued his rapid descent. Both sides of the street were filled with children and at every corner were strewn the rinds of prickly pears. The heads of women were bobbing out of the small windows. The houses looked clean from the outside. How many millions of gallons of paint and whitewash did they splash over these houses, putting more and more weight on them, not to mention the weight of all the storehouses that hold this paint?

This poor rock, how patient and long-suffering it is! It must surely have moaned in pain all these years from the heavy weight thrust upon its shoulders. It won't be long before it cries out in protest in its own way. First a tremor, then a mild shaking, and everyone will understand what it's trying to say. All the citizens of Constantine will then realize the grave error that they have committed.

He stepped aside and let pass a man who was leading a woman shrouded in a long, black veil. No doubt a fiancee he's brought back with him from Europe, he murmured to himself. Then he recalled words that were attributed to Musailama the Imposter:[1] 'O frog, daughter of a frog, croak all you want! You live half in water and half on soil. But you have no power in the water nor over those who come to drink!'

He spat at the couple after they passed him and continued on his way until he reached another open space on his left. He stopped to survey the area, then changed direction. On his left was a narrow lane. At the corner stood a young girl about ten years old. She was light-skinned and wore a lot of makeup. She was staring at him shamelessly.

My poor deceased wife Aisha was about that age when I married her. She looks a lot like her except that my wife didn't wear all that makeup. The Prophet himself, prayers and peace upon him, married Aisha when she was only nine. He wanted to tell his people that female charm begins at birth . . .

A good Muslim will spend eternity in Paradise deflowering virgins, according to a prophetic tradition. God will reward His servants with what He deprived them of on earth. I want Him to grant me children. May every virgin I deflower give birth to twins. Almighty God alone can make that happen. Heaven will be totally flat, no doubt. It won't be sitting on top of a rock like Constantine.

The audacity of this little girl in makeup is indeed disturbing. God damn her and the Devil. It wouldn't take much to entice her away from here. A girl from this quarter would do anything to get married. If someone proposed, she'd accept in an instant, afraid that someone else might come along and take her place.

He looked to the right and noticed the shell of a large building, lodged between dilapidated houses and the bank of the river. He decided to go down towards the wall which was riddled with holes every few yards. Cautiously, he descended until he got very close to it.

The great ravine where the dark water runs slowly is frightening. Some of the rocks look as though they're ready to crumble. Not even the houses located on the east side of this rock would fill up this huge expanse.

---

1. Contemporary of the Prophet Muhammad who claimed prophethood for himself.

He raised his head and looked out into the distance. There was the forest, the Mansoura Plateau and the Sidi Mabrouk Road. What an island of greenery! Whatever made these people leave such a place and come here in droves?

Down below at the edge of the ravine is the old tobacco factory. It still has the old sign, *Ben Chicou* . . . The students' dormitory. They laid the cornerstone and the place was overrun with students from the Ibn Badis Institute, and then all of a sudden the war broke out. Slowly the place began to empty until neither a student nor a teacher was left. If the war hadn't come so quickly, we would have finished the fourth floor of the building. Things don't always turn out the way you expect them to! There are buildings that are hard to identify. Ah, there's that damned building with the *No Smoking* sign posted on the front in French and Arabic. That's the fuel depot.

The granary is at the Qantara Gate, the electric company is at Sidi M'sid and the fuel depot is at Sidi Rashid. The city is equipped to be self-sufficient for at least several months. When the rock shakes and the earthquake starts to be felt, the fuel depot will fall into the Rhumel Valley and its oil will spill out. A great fire will ignite and spread throughout all the warehouses in the city and its flames will rise up to the highest skies. As long as there's a bottom, as long as there's a world in turmoil, there will be a constant threat to the city. Sidi M'sid takes up the upper part of the city while Sidi Rashid takes up the lower part. Nothing will remain except that which is written on the pages of history, on the eternal tablet, of the crimes which were committed.

He took another look out on the ravine and felt his head spin. He closed his eyes and then opened them. The pigeons were flying serenely around him. They hold such a strong attraction. Their flying is most majestic when they do it way up in the sky. But when they fly below, around the ravine, especially when seen from above, it seems as though they fly with great effort, under duress.

Over yonder you can see a part of the Sidi Rashid Bridge, sitting on top of arches fortified by rocks and cement. It valiantly resists the heavy carts and enormous trucks that trample on it. However awesome the earthquake may be, however strong and mighty, this bridge will never collapse. It will surely remain a bridge, even if the river below it ceases to flow or all of its foundations crumble. It's a bastion of men's insistence on being defiant and arrogant. More than that, it is a symbol of their ardent desire to participate in creation. Whoever finds himself on top of the bridge when the rock shakes and the city melts will have the best chance to be saved. The Lord, through the intercession of Sidi Rashid, will no doubt inspire His pious servants to gather on top of the bridge. At the time of the earthquake, every important landowner, factory owner, merchant and imam will find himself standing on the Sidi Rashid Bridge, exactly at the right moment.

He felt a bit more comfortable, took several steps backward, then turned around and headed back. He saw the girl with the made-up eyes and the flashing teeth. He leered at her. She had firm young breasts and a slender waist. She had a round, curvaceous rump, ample thighs and long, shapely legs. 'A house that used to shelter one family now shelters ten,' he thought. These people must sleep on top of one another. Everything is turned upside down in this city.

'It's a dead-end street, uncle.'

'Then how do I get to Sidi Rashid?' he asked the young boy who cautioned him against going down. He stopped long enough to wait for an answer. His eyes glanced up and down at the walls. None of the lanes and alleyways has a name, nor are there those distinctive odours you find everywhere else. There's absolutely no character, no distinction to this place. Everything looks the same. '*There's only Hallaj in my jubba.*'[1]

This is what happens to every netherworld. It deteriorates, crumbles and dissolves, until nothing of it remains except its low-liness.

'Go up straight ahead and turn left at the first alleyway. Walk along

---

1. Reference to the line: '*Ma fi jubbati ghayra allah*' (There is only God in my *jubba*), attributed to the famous mystic al-Hallaj who was executed in 922.

Corneille Street until you come to a vacant lot. Then ask again when you get there.'

At the foot of the bridge, underneath its massive arches and behind the launderette operated by the prostitutes, sits the shrine and mosque of Sidi Rashid, hidden from the rest of the world. At one time it must have stood at the top of a high hill, then it started to fall down slowly until it reached ground level. How could any of God's saints take up residence in such a netherworld!

What brought me to this place? What am I doing here? I must be out of my mind, muttered Shaykh Abdelmajid Boularwah as he stood in front of a door that was painted dark green . . .

You came to pray at the tomb of Sidi Rashid . . .

But since when do I believe in tombs and shrines? I fought against them alongside our great reformist thinker, Ibn Badis. I called on the people to reject them. It's nothing more than an adoration of tombs, a kind of heresy started by the common people.

No, sir!

You believed in them all along, even when you preached against them from the pulpit. They're part of a great heritage that is like the great rock of Constantine. If you pull one stone out from underneath, the whole thing will collapse. To question customs, traditions and even superstitions leads to questioning the whole basis of life. It's like blasphemers who exploit the outcries of sincere men of learning and religion only to become more blasphemous in their thinking.

You never even agreed with Ibn Badis.

You used to think, and you still think, that whatever binds people to God should be considered lawful and legal, even if it included idolatry. You didn't express your opinion openly, but you believed in it fervently.

Telling people to refrain from visiting the shrines of learned and pious men would be the same as telling them to stop being patient with what God does to them, which, in the end, is telling them to revolt against poverty. Religion is one whole, it doesn't come in pieces to be picked at and chosen. Everything that binds the common people to God and to the past is religion. Any attempt to separate religion from the past, from the days, months, years and centuries, and all that was created, developed and implanted in their thinking, is an assault on religion itself.

Our glorious ancestors put an end to the Mu'tazilites[1] and the rationalist thinkers so effectively that it seems as though these two groups never existed at all. Our ancestors defended the positions of Abu Musa al-Ash'ari[2] and built schools of law based upon his views. So let his views live on. History has recorded Mu'awiya's victory over Ali,[3] so what use would it be to go back and argue the point about Ali's caliphate? The road has been paved by our orthodox ancestors. Any attempt to question the past would only allow the apostates, heretics and blasphemers to obstruct it.

'Let me go and perform my prayers at the shrine of Sidi Rashid.'

Shaykh Abdelmajid Boularwah blurted out his decision to pray and then pushed himself through the green door. Behind it was a large cement courtyard. At the other end, on the left side of the entrance, was the mosque behind which was a door which looked as though it could be a residence, then another door which definitely was a residence. Two elderly women were sitting on the doorstep. One of them was busy picking through green wheat, sitting next to a large pot and several glasses.

'Did you come to make a visit?' asked the other woman as she jumped to her feet.

'Yes.'

1. A sect of freethinkers who came into existence in eighth-century Basra (Iraq) and whose belief in free will and predestination earned them a reputation, among the more orthodox Muslims, as a sect of schismatics.

2. Abu Musa al-Ash'ari was a companion of the Prophet who played a dubious role in the arbitration between 'Ali and Mu'awiyah following the battle of Siffin (657). He should not be confused with his more famous descendant Abu al-Hasan al-Ash'ari, a one-time Mu'tazilite who returned to orthodox Islam and founded a school of scholastic theology (d. c. 940).

3. Cousin and son-in-law of the Prophet whom some believe he designated as his successor, a claim which was at the origin of the schism between Sunni and Shi'a Islam.

'Then please come with me. Sidi Rashid is right over here.'

His attention was caught by a painting of a giant mounted on a horse whose ghoul-like head was being severed by the sword of Sidi Ali. He raised his eyebrows in total disapproval, then cracked a smile.

There's no quibbling in matters of religion, so what harm does this picture do? It merely strengthens people's belief that the enemies of God will perish no matter how strong or gigantic they may be. Even those who do not support Ali's claim to be the successor of the Prophet Muhammad see him as a hero. They dethroned him as caliph and crowned him hero. The masses are like children. They like things plain and simple. If they break something, they want to replace it with something else so that they can forget the pain of loss.

I remember questioning a shaykh at the Zaytouna Mosque in Tunis as he was explaining the conditions of fasting. He said that breaking a fast consisted of three things: entering the throat, settling into the stomach and nourishing the body.

'Then smoking doesn't violate the rules of fasting since it doesn't meet the last two conditions.'

'Anything that doesn't meet these three conditions is not considered a violation of the fast, according to the Maliki school of Islamic law.'

'Then why don't the common people know this?'

'Because they can't intellectualize it. And most importantly because they can't refrain from smoking!'

The mosque is very small, maybe one hundred square feet in all. The pulpit on the left is plain and simple, and the tomb is on the right. Machine-made carpets cover the ceiling, walls and floor. A few brass lamps are hanging here and there, but no electricity seems to be flowing to them. Perhaps someone forgot to take care of that. There are a few candles by the tomb, which is covered in old green cloth.

The old woman was following him closely as though she were guarding the treasures of Sidi Rashid against thieves. He then faced the pulpit and started to pray:

O, Sidi Rashid, Saint of God, I've spent nine hours on the road, coming from the capital, in this intense heat for a matter that not only concerns me greatly but concerns all pious people to whom God has bequeathed His land. I will not hide from you, for indeed you know all things that lie deep within the souls of men, that I came here to outwit the government in its attempts to seize control of my land. I want to register my property in the names of my relatives with the stipulation that they gain access to it and reap the benefits of it only after I'm dead. But my problem, O Saint of God, is that I haven't been able to locate any of them. The first one died as a martyr in the war for independence. The second is a high-ranking officer with power and influence. And officers, as you know, Sidi Rashid, even if they don't share the views of the government or have any faith in its policies, are for some inexplicable reason faithful to it. Even if there were officers who did care about wealth and influence, they wouldn't pursue it in agriculture. They are much more interested in big business projects and modern technology. The third relative, oh, the third one, what can I say? He was the paragon of the family, the one destined for Paradise. He was a pious ascetic, a custodian at the shrine of Sidi Abdelmu'min. But . . . he became, how can I say this . . . he became a communist. He goaded the workers to strike and brainwashed the poor students with his subversive ideas and forced the government into implementing godless, satanic projects and policies.

I pledge to make a large offering to you, O Sidi Rashid. I will light a candle, a whole box of candles, if you stop this project and safeguard our land, for me and all your righteous servants.

It is not enough to sway them with gifts, Sidi Rashid, since their hearts are full of rancour. You can't offer any advice either, since their heads swell with conceit and arrogance. There are only two solutions, as far as I can tell: first, that the fires of civil unrest consume them, and second, that a great earthquake strike all the rabble who intend to profit from our land.

'I pledge to you, Sidi Rashid, a large offering.'

'An offering?' asked the old woman as she opened the door for him.

'I've made a pledge. I'll come back when Sidi Rashid answers my prayer.'

He left the mosque in a hurry and headed up the street towards the bridge. He felt as if a tremendous load was lifted from his mind.

That little girl wearing all that makeup arouses me. I forgot to ask Sidi Rashid to grant me offspring. I still haven't decided to remarry. I think I will. I'll marry a young girl. I'll marry that young thing, standing by the door, all made-up in lipstick and eye shadow.

I pledge to Sidi Rashid a box of candles every year, one for every child she bears for me.

Ah, the end of this tiresome metal stairway! The Sidi Rashid Bridge makes one forget that awesome chasm that lies between us and the earth.

Down below is Remblai Street as it always was. There's the hardware store that sells everything imaginable. Men and women of all ages sit amid the smoke coming out of the ovens from the bakery. They carry all kinds of bags, nylon, paper, cloth, that hold their belongings: old keys, crooked nails, broken taps, tattered clothes and worn-out shoes. Scraps of dirty bread and prickly pear skins are scattered all over the place.

Up above are Camels' Square and Souiqa. The whole quarter resembles the kasbah of Old Algiers turned upside down. The tiles on the rooftops look as though they were put there in the time of Noah. It looks more like an old worn-out, worm-eaten carpet. The walls look as though they're about to cave in. There are lots of houses that are falling apart, houses that are totally abandoned and houses that lean against one another. The terraces have been invaded by cats, some sleeping, others prowling about, still others staring into space. Next to them sit television antennas, some pointing towards the north, others south, east and west. Many of the window panes are cracked. The faces of women are peering through some of them, while others have pitchers sitting on their sills, with water seeping through their cracks. In some window panes jasmine flowers are growing out of tomato crates and geraniums in clay pots. In some places you can see clusters of red peppers hanging on the walls; elsewhere the peppers are green.

They water the graves in the cemeteries and plant flowers on top of their dead. This is all one big cemetery here and pretty soon Sidi Rashid is going to enlarge it by turning the place upside down. Not even the customary odours bother to invade this place. The cars are all racing one another as though the drivers don't trust the bridge. Here people practically live on top of one another. Most of them are old women and men.

The old theatre is up ahead, just behind the main square. Next to it are the post office and the former headquarters of the French National Guard. If you look just a little bit to the left, right after the Cirta Hotel, you will see high-rise buildings with big windows and drab colours, surrounded on all sides by eucalyptus trees. If you look long enough, you can envision the shape of a crescent moon in which you can see patches of golden straw and red earth, some construction sites and bare hills, all blending together as they stretch out towards the horizon.

If you look carefully at the land, whether it be already sown or ready for planting, you feel a certain peace of mind, knowing that God's blessings still abound among His pious servants and that His mercy is still bestowed upon them. You feel secure in the fact that all sins are forgiven except those that these heretics commit on the land in violation of God's law.

The land belongs to those who own it, who have always owned it, and no one else. Ownership of property is like talent, intelligence, genius. It doesn't come to just anyone. Land is land and that's all. Owning it is no big deal. It goes beyond the question of rich or poor, satiation or hunger, profit and yield.

Land is land.

Our ownership of it means more than simply owning land. It's a question of honour, majesty and power which elevates you to the level of prophets and men of God, high above those who don't own any at all. Ah, but those thieves understand land in terms of market value. They see land through communist, materialist eyes. They see it in terms of rich and poor, landowner and sharecropper, harvests to be exported for hard currency and oppressive taxes that they can impose on it.

I pledge to you, Sidi Rashid, a large offering. Act quickly. The kindest gift is the one given with no forethought. Ignite the devouring fires of civil unrest and bring on the horrific earthquake. Get rid of the government, the poor people, the workers, students and unionists. Rebuild a new nation, populated only by us, the noble classes, people of good stock.

He started to feel all of a sudden a certain tightness, a heaviness and gloom. He quickened his pace as he continued to walk. He was still muttering to himself:

There's still the sieve-maker and the saddler. These two will never be officers, martyrs or communists. There's no way they could have changed jobs. I don't think so; at least, I hope not. But who knows, these days that are nearing the end of the world?

Shaykh Boularwah finally came to the end of the bridge.

On the left is the old National Guard building, a gas station and a road that goes down a hill where you can find a stand for taxis coming and going to Annaba. At the corner is the coffee shop and on the right is a big stand for sweets and perfumes. The entrance to Remblai Street and other smaller lanes that lead into the square are just behind that.

To think that people in this city still need perfume!

The cars were moving up and down the street from every direction. He turned towards the right and looked ahead. Bounab Ali Street. The cinema is still there. There are chicken feathers everywhere. Ah, over there is a greasy-spoon café. The old familiar stenches are starting to come back. An old woman with an arm full of bread is sitting against a wall talking in a loud voice to someone who can't be seen:

'I'm telling you, sister, that their bread is dried out. It's only good for dipping into a stew. But what's important is that they give it to us, may God reward them! The living put the head of the dead wherever they wish. What I was saying is that her son was killed at the

Boulfarayis dump and she herself was wounded in the chest and the arm. She was still holding a can of sardines and the only thing that they thought to do was to hack her arm off with a cleaver.'

Old people, men and women, stand along the walls, up and down the sidewalks. Students pace the pavement, trying to make some money by writing amulets, reading palms and telling fortunes.

An old woman's voice could be heard above the din:

'Please, sir, my oldest son, the apple of my eye, the only thing I have in the world, signed up to go to France. He bought a ticket for the ferry and he's waiting his turn to go. Please write an amulet that will keep him from going. Do this one thing for me, I implore you. The poor thing has no luck or else he would've found a job like his friends. Write something that will bring him good luck.'

'He won't go. Even if his turn comes up, he'll miss the boat. Your son will stay with you, my dear woman.'

Next to them was a woman covered in a veil who was crouched down beside another student.

'Twelve men came and asked for her hand in marriage, but none of them actually came through. She's not one-eyed, nor has she been tampered with, if you know what I mean. My daughter is beautiful. She can sew, make clothing and embroider. Her hands are magic. What's wrong is that the first man who came to ask for her hand backed down at the last minute and married a neighbour.'

'She'll marry the thirteenth suitor, God willing!'

'If only you could bring back the eleventh one, that would be best. His mother isn't alive, so they'd have a place to live.'

'Then she'll marry the eleventh one, God willing!'

Right next to them was yet another student who was reading a newspaper. A middle-aged man dressed in Moroccan clothing was sitting beside him and, like the old bedouin soothsayers, was telling fortunes by drawing lines and circles in sand which he spread out on a piece of cloth. He was talking to a young man from the village:

'I see green; there's green in front and behind you. Go ahead, make a wish and try your luck. Between you and good fortune is a serpent with seven heads. You are also being followed by a Jewish evil genie who has seven souls. Try your luck and see if I cut off the serpent's head and chop off the genie's feet. Whatever trip you're planning, postpone it. She'll come back to you! Don't budge from where you are because you're going to receive a notice from the government that will make you very happy.'

God help us, Sidi Rashid, he's going to receive nothing at all.

Shaykh Abdelmajid Boularwah was muttering to himself as he continued to walk down the street. He wondered what on God's earth had brought him to this awful situation. He felt like a tourist. He looked up and saw a sign that said *National Liberation Front: Bureau of Information and Propaganda* and was painted in red and green lettering on a white poster.

Just then he overheard another conversation:

'Write, write to the president himself, if you must. Tell him that Issa Boushu'ayr, who was with you up in the mountains, has been wronged, treated unjustly. Like all decent men, he got married four years ago, but the marriage didn't work out. So, like anyone else, he divorced his wife, brought her back to her father's home and left her there. She sued him and they forced him to give her a hundred dinars in a settlement. It's not a big sum, but poor Issa doesn't work. He can't even read or write. But Issa Boushu'ayr is a holy warrior, so he can't degrade himself and accept just any job. Issa forgot the matter just like anybody in his place would. Four years later, he receives a summons from the government. They sentence him to four years in jail and fine him five hundred dinars as a penalty.

'Write to him, say that you know me. I was with you in the mountains during the war. Tell him: if you don't find me at my address, if you don't act quickly, then you'll find me in jail.'

My relative the saddler is at Wool Market Square and the other one, the sieve-maker, is at Bardo. I'll start at Bardo since it's closer to here.

So Shaykh Abdelmajid Boularwah decided. He turned abruptly to the left, trying to escape from all those voices on Bounab Ali Street, voices that were shrieking in the ears of the passers-by and were particularly grating to those like himself who chanced to be innocently walking by.

FOUR

Majaz al-Ghanam
(The Bridge at Flock Crossing)

Shaykh Abdelmajid Boularwah was dismayed that his foray into Bounab Ali Street was in vain. So he decided to go along Shitour Umar Street behind the post office where he suddenly found himself facing a long line of young people standing on the right side of the street. A voice coming out of a loudspeaker was calling out their full names.

He stepped back and looked on disdainfully. He then focused his attention on a sign that read: *Bureau of Labour Unions.* He studied the faces of the young men but saw nothing at all in them. Their glances were fixed and far away. Their voices were calm and their movements composed. You could say that they were sitting pathetically by death's door. Start here, Sidi Rashid, with this building and this rabble.

An officer came out of the doorway, down the stairs and headed up the street. Shaykh Boularwah stopped and thought about waiting for him.

I'll ask him about Tahir Boularwah. He must know him. Tahir Boularwah is the only hope for my salvation, for the salvation of all landowners, who are honourable and pious people. I'll register all of my land under his name and put him in contact with the other landowners. I'll make you an offering for his help, Sidi Rashid. He must succeed in the scheme, which is more important than the earthquake, more important than any catastrophic civil strife. No, I won't ask him. I'll ask my cousin, Adbelqadir, about him. He must surely be in contact with him.

My teaching profession has kept me from managing my holdings properly. It's just that this great tension within me, between my being a scholar and a businessman, as Shaykh Idir would say, never allowed me to establish close ties to my family. I always hoped that I would have my own children who could help me manage my affairs, but things don't always turn out the way we want them to. I'll have to start all over again. In fact, now is the right time to get serious. Teaching and supervising a major educational institution is not a bad line of work, after all. We have to fight the enemy with every weapon. In my high school we work continuously to undermine heresy and moral corruption. We train young people to qualify one day for positions of leadership in all walks of life. Besides, they'll be entering universities and will come face to face with hordes of communists. I wonder what they're all doing here.

'What are they doing here?' he shouted out to an old man leaning against the wall of the café.

'They're here to report to the Board of Medical Examiners. These young men in the National Service will be building the road to the Sahara.'

He made no comment and continued on his way downhill. He stared at the sign of the café and wondered what *Office of Social Classification*, written in gold lettering, meant. He looked inside. There was quite a display of local citizenry from different age groups. There were older men sitting across from young men who were embracing their girlfriends shamelessly. Apart from their ages, nothing seems to distinguish the professions or social classes of these people. And from the looks of them, nothing seems to distinguish their wallets either.

They're all in a stupor, dazed and confused even about their own affairs. They seem as though they're hovering under the shadow of some horrid nightmare or drifting on a big raft, which might at any moment be sucked down to the bottom of the deep, dark sea.

He entered a garden where the flowers were starting to bloom and the trees stood majestically tall. Despite the oppressive humidity, there was a bustling crowd of people.

Even here they peddle their goods!

There was a young boy with a pail of soaking chickpeas. Sitting across from him was a middle-aged man with a crate of dates. Just above his head was a sign that read: *Do not sit on the fence.* A boy with a bucket of prickly pears was waving a knife, threatening a group of kids standing around him. There were stone benches full of people of all ages and appearances. A tea vendor stood in the middle of the crowd, boiling water in a big kettle on top of an old-fashioned brazier. A second, third and even fourth tea vendor, keeping busy in their soiled village clothing, were waving their hands back and forth, passing out glasses of tea and taking them back. A photographer with an antique camera set up his equipment in a corner of the garden. Naturally, there was another photographer, a third and even a fourth. Hundreds of bicycles of every shape and size were scattered throughout the garden.

In every corner of this city there's some kind of trading. There's a buyer and a seller in every place you set foot. As expected, there's the thief and the pickpocket as well. The Prophet gave his blessings to trade, but of course he never had in mind this sordid kind of trade. This is more begging than trade!

O Lord, withhold Your blessings from these people and their wicked profiteering and rid us of them forever. They abandoned their villages and deserts and came to the city only to feign poverty and beg for the government's mercy.

He cut through several smaller streets and headed in the direction of the Cirta Hotel.

From the outside, it looks very modest, but what could it possibly look like inside? I wonder if any Algerians ever patronize it and what sort they are. Tahir Boularwah must surely stay here whenever he passes through town.

Leaning on the wall of the hotel, he turned towards the Ministry of Agriculture. The paintings on the buildings disgusted him. Instead of painting carriages, horses and horsemen, they had to draw pictures of harvesters, tillers and woodcutters. How fond the colonizers, the aghas and the pashas must have been of these drawings, here in this well-fortified citadel of theirs, where I could never set foot. No, I was much too poor for those who came here on a regular basis. But, nevertheless, I did have solid connections with my colonialist neighbours who frequented places like this.

May you go to hell, Ibn Khaldoun. You are a blasphemer, not a historian. You are one shrewd heretic who found a very clever way to propagate your heresy without getting hurt.

He muttered to himself as he walked down the street. Directly after the hotel a row of one-storey houses begins. To the left there is a wall all along the street that divides Bardo from Kudiya. At the corner you find the Shining Stars Café, the preferred stopping place for the drivers of the city buses. The Thousand and One Nights Café, from where you hear the slamming of domino chips, is next to it.

That old man with the snub nose has no qualms playing with all these young boys:

'Waiter.'

'Coming right away.'

'Coffee.'

'Tea.'

'One Benharoun.'

'Pay up, first.'

'No, we're still on the first round,' said the old snub-nosed man.

'Hurry, Sidi Rashid, hurry!' murmured Shaykh Abdelmajid Boularwah.

Suddenly a clamour erupted from another corner of the café.

'Throw in your chips.'

'By God, I will not.'

'Then it's over. That's against the rules.'

'I dropped one of the chips.'

'Then restack. You're playing like someone from Setif.'

'Setif or Annaba. You still have to pay for the drinks, whether you like it or not.'

He stamped his feet and quickened his pace.

A whole box of candles, Sidi Rashid. Algeria's desert is indeed vast. If Tahir Boularwah has become what I want him to be, he will banish all those who don't own a shop or hold a position or land or work in a factory or farm. The owner of that closed shop couldn't find any name for it other than *Jaziya Clothing*, probably named after some beautiful woman. Ah, that luxurious mosque. How remarkable!

He stopped to look at it, but his ear caught the sound of a low voice:

'It used to be a cinema. He bought it from a Frenchman for a song. But when the government issued a decree nationalizing all the cinema houses, it hurt him badly. The miserable bastard never found the way to voice his objections, except to turn it into a mosque.'

He was wise to do it, whispered Shaykh Abdelmajid to himself.

The low voice continued:

'As long as he was stuffing the profits into his pockets, he never thought about turning it into a mosque. But then when he saw that it was going to be turned into either a school, hospital or factory, he decided to freeze the assets. But he wasn't content to do just that. He had to go and open his mouth and declare that he didn't mind giving up some of his major holdings, but that nationalization and socialism were what he was against.'

'He's a hero,' muttered Shaykh Boularwah, as one of the two younger men standing near him commented:

'Even the government let itself be duped by such tricks. God give it guidance.'

Shaykh Abdelmajid Boularwah turned in their direction and gave them a dirty look. When they saw him they moved away. He found himself staring at a sign on a wall opposite him that led up a flight of stairs onto a main road. The sign read: *Grammont Bill 1850: It is unlawful to abuse animals.* He looked in the direction of the mosque. He smiled, then resumed his walk downward as he looked at other signs on the walls: *Chantilly Brothers: Travel Agency: Constantine, Ain Baida, Khanshia, Tebessa, Sedrata* and *Township of Constantine: Department of Water and Public Utilities.*

I'll take a short cut here on the left, he decided, but then suddenly stopped.

'Police, police!' yelled someone from the crowd.

Gangs of young boys shot out from all directions, running away and carrying utensils, spools of cloth, packages of meat, cleavers and knives. A police car whizzed by without stopping as the young boys kept on running, racing each other to get to a secure place. The screaming grew louder as the crowd of boys thickened. There were even grown-ups running along in the confusion. In the midst of it all a young boy fell to the ground with a knife in his stomach and blood flowing in the street.

'He fell on his knife.'

'Someone pushed him.'

'He's going to die.'

'That's for sure.'

'Stop a car and get him to a hospital.'

'Ammar tripped him.'

'No, it was Boujum'a.'

'No, he fell on his own.'

'I've got seven sheep's heads. Do you want to buy some?'

'Not me. I've got twenty tripes I've got to get rid of.'

'Look, he's dead.'

The boys disappeared with their stolen meat and only the boy lying on the ground with the knife in his stomach dripping with blood was left behind. A crowd of old men and women gathered around him. Shaykh Boularwah spat in disgust. Deep down he felt glad. He continued on his way, walking down the stone pavement taking wide steps.

As he walked, he was assaulted by a strong, putrid odour. He looked to see where it was coming from. On the grounds of a municipal building there was a pool of stale, brackish water. On the left was a barbed-wire fence that surrounded a huge military barracks. Half of it was being used by the army while the other half had been made into a warehouse for storing food.

Even here there is a warehouse!

The street extends on the right-hand side. There are houses of mud brick covered with sheets of corrugated tin and corrugated tin houses covered with mud. There are several residential units in the area. Scraps of paper, blocks of wood and sheets of tin pollute the streets and sidewalks. Rusty water gushes out from all sides, forming little streams that all seem to come together at the top of the street.

When Sidi Rashid chooses the second solution and shakes this rock free of all these people and their wicked, sinful ways, he won't have to exert much effort. All it will take will be for one of the Kudiya buildings to topple over these shacks and smash them. Then these streams of water will flush them all into the Rhumel Valley.

Three unveiled women suddenly came out of an alley. They walked down the street, looking as though they had a long way yet to go. He stared at them from the corner of his eye.

Still in their prime, but they look so gaunt, with dark complexions and puffy eyes. One of them was wearing trousers, another a loose flowing dress and the third a skirt above her thighs.

'He said we're going to Oran. We'll stay there a week and then come back.'

'I'm not going anywhere!'

'What's holding you here in this cemetery? One beer costs more than water from the Zemzem well in Mecca.'

'But we have no idea who his two friends are.'

'So why should that bother you. Why do you care?'

'I'm not going anywhere out of Constantine, especially during the wedding season.'

'So you dance all night long for a measly ten bucks that'll only end up in your pimp's pocket. Come with us to Oran for a few days. It'll do you good to get away and relax.'

Just at the moment that the three women were about to pass Shaykh Boularwah, one of them started to sing in a loud voice:

'O, good neighbour, Hammoud, come and do with me as you please!'

A whiff of expensive perfume filled his lungs and he lowered his eyes as they passed him. The scent of the perfume started to fade away and a nauseating stench replaced it. He looked up and right in front of him were black spots that covered part of the dirt road and the two sides of the street. He looked more closely and made out that they were goat skins. He recalled the scene of the boy lying on the street with the knife in his stomach and the other boys waving their hands with the meat, knives and cleavers. He spat and continued on his way.

If it weren't a matter of such urgency, I never would have budged from the capital. Or at least, I would stop to rest in a hotel until tomorrow. But that's impossible. You should never put off until tomorrow what you can do today. Getting ahead of the government is no easy matter. Belbey says that I'm too late. It's true that I should have started earlier, but it's not too late. The problem is that I'm not just a farmer! I'm a director of a school and a scholar as well. I've been forced to be negligent but not really negligent, more like being careless, heedless. My good intentions, unfortunately, were misplaced. And then they deceived us! They're all two-faced hypocrites.

What's important, though, is that I'm here. With any luck I'll find my cousin Abdelqadir the sieve-maker. I can imagine him having seven or eight kids. I'll make an agreement with him and register my land in each of their names. Of course, priority goes to my nephew Tahir, the high-ranking officer with all the influence and connections. But where can I find him? Abdelqadir will definitely point me in his direction. Had I known that Tahir Boularwah the pickpocket would climb to such a high rank, I would have lent him that sum of money when he asked for it right on the spot! But what can a man do? Money doesn't grow on trees and money spent never comes back. Furthermore, trade is not an easy business and Tahir never had any training in it. I was right not to trust him. I'm his uncle and I owe it to him not to give him any reason to resent me.

'My good man, a tractor factory is a great accomplishment, at least that's what they're saying.'

'It's true that it would benefit Constantine, since it is the agricultural centre for all of eastern Algeria.'

'These matters are being studied very seriously, as they should be, by the best engineers and scientists. Algeria is moving forward!'

'What can I say, one way or the other? One hand builds and ten others destroy. The state builds a factory and the sons of bitches ruin it with bribery and nepotism.'

'What's important . . .'

Quickening his pace, he passed them as they continued their conversation.

The sun is so strong that the darkness is coming back to me. When the earthquake comes, the Hotel Panorama will fall right here. The earth underneath it will give way and it'll all come tumbling down. The factory that those two were talking about weighs heavily on the rock just like everything else and it makes the rock lose its balance.

These imbeciles . . .

Suddenly he found himself in front of a drab, grey building whose stories seemed almost indistinguishable. Strings of peppers, old rags and broken utensils hung from the windows. This is the quarter's skyscraper, towering high above the Hotel Panorama.

No doubt the residents of this quarter take turns living in this building. They left it a dull grey so that no one from the neighbouring quarter would want to live in it. Not a soul in the entire area would even look at it except for the residents of the Hotel Panorama quarter. It makes sense. Painting it any other colour would make the people of this slum feel their own misery and grief. Water seeks its own level, as they say.

I'm almost there. I'll turn left at this building and fifty yards away will be the shop. Poor Abdelqadir. I haven't seen him since the incident. No doubt he'll grill me as soon as he sees me.

At the corner of the street, he caught the tail end of a conversation between two older men who were speaking in the accent of his own village:

'But it's a source of great pride, my friend. A real gem in our fair city of Constantine.'

'In all of Algeria.'

'Built with donations from the people.'

'But the authorities coerced the people into donating.'

'Islam is still alive.'

'Thank God for that.'

'But what bothers me is the name, Prince Abdelqadir Mosque! Prince Abdelqadir?!'

'You're right! The title "Prince" is too much. Sidi Abdelqadir would have been more appropriate.'

'What counts is that our government abide by our religion and choose men who are pious and God-fearing.'

'Scram!' sneered Shaykh Abdelmajid as he passed them by. He stopped a few moments to think . . .

Not one soul from this miserable quarter of yours will enter heaven. Neither prayer nor fasting will win you God's acceptance. Your religion will be no use to you. You won't even earn a place in hell. You'll be considered animals and insects. Neither God and his angels nor the angels of damnation will have time to waste giving any thought to the likes of you. Some of you will be thrown into heaps with dogs and others with flies. And your children will end up with cats and goats. Scram! The two of you talk about the government and lavish praise on it. One of you is taken by a tractor factory and the other by the Prince Abdelqadir Mosque. And another, God knows what he likes. Maybe it's unions or communism or even prisons. When you're all in the desert at Ain Salih or Adrar or in the mountains at Haggar, then give us your opinions about the government, you miserable fools. You incur the wrath of the wealthy by your mere presence and your silly chatter.

'Peace and greetings upon you.'

Shaykh Boularwah spoke as he stood in front of a shop from which the strong smell of roasting meat was escaping. There was a young

man standing behind the fire and the shaykh stared at him contemptuously.

Maybe that's his son. How could he possibly have a drop of our
blood running through his veins? You can never tell in these wicked
times of impending doom. Maybe he's just renting the place.

'Where is Abdelqadir?'

'Which Abdelqadir?'

'The owner of the place.'

'I'm the owner of the place.'

'Since when?'

'I've been here since independence.'

'Do you have any idea where the man who was here before you has
gone?'

'No one's left here, uncle. Even before independence, even before
the French and the Jews left, the people divided up their houses and
their businesses. But before they even had a chance to settle in, the
people from the countryside and the villages came in and took over,
along with their relatives and friends. That's the way it goes; one man
picks up and leaves and another settles in.'

'Don't you have any idea where the original owner has gone?'

'Listen, uncle, the Bardo that you see is constantly changing.
Sometimes you'll get a flood or a mudslide or maybe the government
will come and demolish part of it. And then there's always fire.'

'This time there won't be a store left standing!'

'What are you saying?'

'Oh, nothing. I'm saying that the name of the original owner is
Abdelqadir Boularwah. He used to make and sell sieves.'

'That must have been before they rebuilt the quarter.'

'When was the quarter rebuilt?'

'Not all at once. Whenever a part of it deteriorated, they rebuilt it.
There was a Tunisian here before I bought the place. Ah, now I
remember, it was a Tunisian who sold pies.'

'There is no power or strength except in God! Isn't there anyone
here from the old neighbourhood whom I could ask?'

'Let's see, who? Ah, there's Hammana, the saddler. He's the only one who hasn't left. He always said that his trade would be of no use in the city and that he was born here and here he'll remain until he dies.'

'Where's his shop?'

'Right behind that lane over there. He's the only saddler there, anyway.'

Disgusted and fed-up with the incessant chattering and insolent manner of the man grilling the meat, Shaykh Abdelmajid Boularwah left the shop, murmuring to himself about how disrespectfully he spoke, as though he were one of his lowly customers. What a son-of-a-bitch! He's probably roasting dog meat, just like his own kind!

As he continued on his way he came to a fine-looking building and was surprised to find it there. He stopped to get a better look. It was painted in white and blue. What's that sign over there on the wall say? Unbelievable. *Municipal Health Unit!* The town even takes an interest in the health of these people? That's extraordinary! Not only that, there's a school right over there across the street. Will wonders never cease, O Sidi!

Now that's what I call a waste of good money. That's what makes these people corrupt. Instead of giving them work, you give them medicine and education. What could the people of this quarter possibly do if they go to high school or university? They'll end up ruining our religion and the future of generations to come. The children of the poor will mingle with the children of the rich in the same high school or college and they'll receive the same education. Then they'll defy the will of God and rise up in opposition to it. They'll open up the place to outsiders and let their destructive ideas come in and destroy us!

'Good afternoon.'

'Good afternoon, in good health and happiness. You look familiar.'

'I'd like to ask you about a sieve-maker who used to live here many years ago. His shop was over there where the meat griller works.'

'Of course, you two are related. Sidi Abdelqadir, may God protect him and his good name. Please have a seat.'

'Actually, I'm in a rush. I have an urgent mission that I must accomplish as quickly as possible.'

'Please rest a moment on top of this crate. You're all in a sweat. Could I offer you something cold to drink?'

'No, please don't bother. But thank you just the same.'

'As I said, my good sir, Sidi Abdelqadir, may God protect him, must be a relative of yours.'

'He's my cousin.'

'Ah, yes. He spoke to me about a cousin of his. An educated and well-to-do man. Perhaps that's you?'

'As far as the education, well, that's true. But as for the wealth, well, you understand how people, especially relatives, can sometimes exaggerate these things. Whatever happened to my cousin, Abdelqadir?'

'As I told you, my good sir, life goes on and things change. Out of sight, out of mind.'

'Nothing bad has happened to him?'

'On the contrary. Your cousin couldn't read or write, isn't that correct?'

'Yes, that's true.'

'When the war broke out, Abdelqadir took charge of our quarter. He collected donations, arms and medicine, things like that. A year later he and I were both arrested. At first they moved us around quite a bit, from one jail to another, from one location to another. Finally, we ended up at the Barwaqiya camp. While I passed the time playing cards and sewing the other inmates' clothes, he was busy becoming literate. He learned how to read and write. He would even memorize whole books and read poetry. After independence, well, can you imagine what was in store for Abdelqadir after independence?'

Shaykh Abdelmajid Boularwah hesitated for a moment since the question took him by surprise. In fact, it baffled him.

Much as I loathe him, I feel proud. The fact that he can read and write makes absolutely no difference to me. But the fact that he's now one of the educated elite, well that's something else. A prisoner and an educated man. Who knows, maybe he's a minister or an ambassador or a local governor or a high official. What if he has an important position in the party?

'My good man, your cousin Abdelqadir is a professor. He teaches in a high school.'

'A teacher of what? Just like that?'

'Well, no, not just like that. Your cousin Abdelqadir started as a teacher trainee. First he finished his elementary school studies and then earned his high-school diploma. He never gave up the struggle. He went on to university and graduated. Your cousin Abdelqadir is an instructor in a high school. He comes here to see me from time to time. My daughter is one of his students. Sidi Abdelqadir, your cousin, is married with children. Look and see what this war has done, what freedom has done!'

That heavy, viscous liquid suddenly came back and started oozing inside him. He felt a tremendous weight pushing him towards the ground and his heart was swelling up, making it hard for him to breathe. He felt as though a hammer was pounding on his skull. He broke out in a sweat and his lips turned yellowish-green, then blue. He took a long, deep breath.

'Are you all right?' asked the saddler.

He motioned to him with his head and hand that there was nothing to worry about. He said it was just a dizzy spell that had been coming and going since the morning. After all, it's very hot, the city air is polluted and there's so much commotion on the streets.

'Your cousin Abdelqadir lives in one of the faculty apartment buildings in Sidi Mabrouk. You can ask anyone when you get there. They all know him.'

'Thank you, I'd like to get back downtown. Where can I catch the bus?'

'Go down past the clinic, below the Uqba Ibn Nafi School, until you get to the end of the road. When you reach the Bridge at Flock

Crossing, you'll find a bus station. If you just missed it, be patient. Another one will come along soon.'

He passed a mill that was turning in circles. The only donkey that was standing close to it was swatting flies with its tail. Used furniture vendors were shouting out prices for their wares without much luck. Several old women were rolling couscous on one of the narrow street corners. A carpenter was hammering, while another was operating an electric saw. A barber, crouched underneath a tree, was holding two cupping glasses on the neck of an old hunchback. Billows of smoke mixed with the sounds of singing were trickling out from a corner of the street:

'Fancy speech has lost its taste, brilliant words now lie in waste.'

Abdelqadir the sieve-maker, who squandered the land that his father bequeathed to him, is a teacher and he lives in faculty housing! This is really a shock to me. It's an assault. When the barefoot, the naked and the sheep herders build palaces and the servant girl gives birth to her mistress, then the hour of doom will come and something horrendous will afflict the world. 'Every suckling female will forget her suckling, and every pregnant female will discharge her burden, and you will see men drunk, yet it will not be in intoxication . . .' The real earthquake is something everyone will feel, some before, some after, and some while it is actually happening, and its massive force will dump all the mud, gravel and sand into the bottom of the ravine.

O Sidi Rashid, man of miracles, perhaps this is one of your finest miracles. Perhaps you have already responded to those who have petitioned you and thus you have spoken. But this should be punishment for everyone, Sidi Rashid, for those who have come up in life, for those who have fallen and for those who have never left their station. Indeed, the real Earthquake of Doom is less powerful, less formidable than its anticipation.

Poor Belbey, poor Nino. Poor Tahir Boularwah, poor Abdelqadir. Poor me.

Those damned bastards from the government! It's not our land they want so much as they want our souls. They want us to fall into a state of anguish and fear, while they feel compelled to act on behalf of these wicked, miserable, poor people who wallow in the lowliness of the world from which they come. I'm afraid I'm falling into their trap. I feel their oppressive weight even before they pounce on me. Miserable terrorists. Criminals! Pathetic, damned to hell!

The weight of the thing grew heavier inside him. You could even see that dark colour in his eyes. He could no longer see where he was going and for a moment he forgot why he was there. He was so dizzy that he felt as though the earth was moving beneath him.

He leaned against the wall of a school and put one hand on his forehead and the other on his heart. He tried to catch his breath, then opened his eyes to avoid the visions that were overpowering him.

The Sidi Rashid Bridge has the shape of a crescent moon. It starts at the heart of the city and rests on slender but well-fortified arches. When it reaches the Sidi Rashid Mosque, it perches above the river confidently and majestically. At its feet the brightly painted buildings lose their lustre and the great ravine fades in comparison to its splendour. In fact the bridge and the ravine look as though they are engaged in a constant struggle where the ravine tries to bring itself together but the bridge prevents it from succeeding. From above, the ravine looks large, but then it narrows. Below, the dark waters glisten. Just a short distance above is a smaller bridge, teeming with activity, which is used as a footbridge by the residents of Janan Tashniya, a quarter that looks as though it was once part of the section of Bardo but has, for some mysterious reason, been separated from it. Janan Tashniya extends from the foot of the mountain at the bottom of the ravine to the highest point of the Sidi Mabrouk Hills. It goes around the hill and descends abruptly towards the river. From that point the buildings and shanties cease, giving way to hills that are stripped bare of any greenery. Behind that is an old, shrivelled-up 'Roman' quarter. Beyond that is the Bridge at Flock Crossing, which extends a modest sixty feet. It seems that those who built it undoubtedly thought of it as temporary and didn't bother to secure it firmly in its banks. Yet this is the most revealing of all the bridges, clearly indicating that the people of Constantine are perpetually conscious of their imminent doom and must therefore plunder from life whatever pieces they can, in whatever moments remain of their lives.

All along the murky waters of the river children bathe and women keep busy washing everything from wool, shopping sacks and clothes to sheepskins and intestines.

When Sidi Rashid accepts my petition, answers my prayers and opts for the second solution, the great ravine will close up and block the flow of the river. A monstrous dam will be erected and the waters will cease to flow. They will collect in one place, rise up and spill over. They'll uproot trees and wreak havoc on the mud houses and shanties. The banks will wash away. This will be the great deluge. O Lord, destroy the abodes of all the infidels on earth. If you let them remain, they will lead your pious servants astray and they will only beget wicked, heathen children.

The bus arrived and Shaykh Abdelmajid Boularwah barely managed to get himself onto it. He took out a coin and muttered: Qantara Gate. He threw himself onto a seat and rested his head between his hands. He closed his eyes. He wished he could turn the seat around or at least not have to listen to all the voices chattering around him.

'They're going to put up some high-rise buildings in Constantine.'

'The company that does prefabricated construction and has already built several buildings here in the city is going to cover the whole country with new construction.'

'Algeria is really moving forward!'

'Even though France still puts obstacles on our road to progress.'

'Nonsense! If you aren't satisfied by sticking your hand into the pot, you won't get satisfied by licking it.'

'In Vietnam, the Americans are getting a thrashing, just as they deserve.'

'The Vietnamese receive truckloads of arms from the Soviet Union every day.'

'I don't understand the difference between Israel and the Arab states. Israel is a capitalist country and so too are many Arab countries. Israel is an agent of the Americans as are many of the Arab leaders. Israel kills Palestinians and many of the Arab governments are against the Palestinians as well.'

'Of course, you're right. This affront to God's will in the name of religion is unbelievable.'

'But Israel isn't the only problem facing the Arabs. Palestine is not the biggest issue confronting us.'

'I told her to drop him, but she insisted that he would be devastated if she left him. I just don't understand her. She loves him and she hates him. She loves me, too, but she doesn't want to run away with me.'

'Don't bother with her. She's nothing but a tramp. She's only taking advantage of your youth and vitality. She'll cheat on you just as she's doing to him.'

'One day he burst in on us while we were in bed. He was stunned. I jumped out of bed stark naked and grabbed him. I pinned him up against the wall with my hands around his neck. "If you don't like it," I said, "then why don't you divorce her!" You know what she did?'

'What?'

'She picked up a cleaver and attacked me. She screamed at me to leave him alone and that if I didn't take my hands off his neck, she was going to split my head open!'

'She told the investigator that it was her father. He asked her to give him a back rub, then he turned over and took her in his arms. When she went before the judge, she said it was her brother and that it was she who provoked him. Then she retracted her statements and said that it could have been either her father or her brother. She said it could have been either one. She said that it was dark and that she had been asleep. And when she awoke, she discovered that the thing had happened. Maybe it was her father or maybe her brother. It could even have been one of the neighbours' sons.'

'What did the judge do?'

'He sentenced them all to jail, the father, the son, the neighbour's son and the girl.'

'He was waiting in a line, with an empty jerry can in his hand. The line was long, but he wasn't at the end of it. He waited his turn but the line didn't seem to be moving.'

'What was the problem? Did they stop selling?'

'No, hold on. There was a patrol there keeping everybody in order.'

'Was it a military or a civilian patrol?'

'They were either soldiers or police. They're all the same.'

'That's not true. Soldiers are soldiers and police are police.'

'Who cares? This is how it always is in Constantine. Anyway, as I was saying, he turned around and suddenly saw an officer standing in the place of one of the salesmen, filling the can of a friend or acquaintance or taking an order from a young girl or woman. People were looking at each other in shock and indignation, signalling to one another that they knew full well what was going on. But this character, the officer in command, kept right on doing what he pleased. In fact, one of his men came over to help him. No one dared to speak up, except my son who shouted out loud:

'"This is not fair!"

'One of the patrolmen turned around to him and asked:

'"What did you say?"

'"Nothing", answered my son.

'But an officer butted in and said that my son had said something in protest. So the commander asked again:

'"What did you say?"

'My son by now was quite annoyed and he answered:

'"You've come here to maintain order. Yet we've been standing here for four hours in this scorching heat and haven't moved one step forward."

'One of the officers grabbed him by the shirt with one hand and whacked him across the face with the other. His nose started to bleed.

They roughed him up and then brought him to the police van. We haven't seen or heard from him in two months. Not a word!'

'What injustice!'

'We didn't know what to say, so we all kept silent.'

The bus stopped in front of the Café Najma. Shaykh Abdelmajid Boularwah got up from his seat and climbed down onto the sidewalk, muttering to himself.

I should go and perform the afternoon prayer before it's too late. I'll make my ablutions at the bathhouse by the footbridge and pray there. Then I'll pass by Wool Market Square to see what has become of my nephew, the saddler. I no longer feel this great need for any of them, as much as I need to find out what happened to them. I rely only on Sidi Rashid and on my nephew, Tahir Boularwah.

Jisr al-Mis'ad
(The Elevator Bridge)

First the West pounced on us militarily and then they dazzled us with their science and technology.

The rock is eroding. We've been watching it for centuries in utter fear and amazement.

When the West came, they tore apart our caves and tunnels and patched them over with bridges. They displayed their mastery of cement with the bridges at Qantara Gate, Sidi M'sid and Sidi Rashid. Then, as if that wasn't enough to show off their skill, they twisted ropes of steel and built with iron and suspended their bridge in mid-air.

All you people who live on this grand cliff, who never cease to fear it and marvel at its wonders, see how we have conquered it! So trample on it as you may, with your feet or on your horses and carriages. Because, one way or the other, the West will come back and do more destruction to it than they've ever done before. They may fill the cracks with lead to hide their fear of the whole earth shaking and not just this rock. Or perhaps they'll dig holes through the cement and hoist the rock on giant columns that stretch for three thousand feet. They may even suspend it on chains just as they have done with these bridges and build a whole new city underneath. And who knows, they may even link it by magnetic attraction to one of their satellites, leaving it gliding in space between heaven and earth.

And what do we do about it?

We remain crammed together on top of this eroding rock, hoarding oil, sugar, soap, coffee and flour. We procreate incessantly and we buy and sell things that wouldn't be bought or sold anywhere else. We steal from each other at night and sell it all back in the morning. We play dominoes and we pray and we call to prayer, we build mosques. We sing and play tambourines and flutes.

How deep this ravine must be!

At the bottom, the murky waters trickle through the rocks and moss, while the birds hover gloomily over it.

Wherever the eye may fall, it is always met by a sharp angle whose point is always at the lower end, while the two sides ascend farther than the eye can see, but never uniting with the third side.

How deep this ravine must be!

From the tribe of Quraysh, there are those who are descendants of Abraham, although Abraham is not a descendant of anyone. The Arabs are descendants of the tribes of Jurhum, Qahtan and Adi. All of the Arabs, be they from Yemen, Hadramaut, Hira, Nejd, Tihama or Hejaz, are descendants from the Arabized, the pure Arabs and the lost tribes of Arabia.

How deep this ravine must be!

We here in Constantine are Arabs, Berbers, Phoenicians and Byzantines, but we are not the descendants of any of these people.

How deep this ravine must be!

We pledged our allegiance to Abu Bakr and then we went and whispered in the ears of Ali and his partisans.

We pledged our allegiance to Umar and then we killed him.

After him, we made Uthman our caliph and we killed him a million times.

We praise Muʿawiya and we rebuke him.

We establish the schools of Islamic law and we demolish them.

We set out on the path of orthodoxy and we end up led astray by heresy.

At the bottom the murky waters trickle through the rocks and moss while the birds hover gloomily over it.

There are Arabs in Egypt and there are pharaohs in Egypt. There are Arabs in Syria and Iraq as there are Phoenicians, Babylonians,

Hittites, Kurds and Druze. We make the rock heavier and nothing else. We make it lose its balance. Yet the worst thing is that constant feeling in our souls that the earthquake is coming and we can do nothing about it. We sit by and watch in utter fear and amazement.

'May God forgive me,' murmured Shaykh Boularwah over and over again. He felt a pain of despair throbbing in his heart. He stopped and leaned against a nearby wall as he contemplated the bridge and the ravine beneath it.

I have this premonition that tells me that there will be a violent storm tonight. So I'll do my ablutions, perform the dusk prayers and then look for Rizqi, the saddler, near Wool Market Square. Then I'll leave town. I have no intention of spending the night here.

He thought to himself, but instead of leaving the place where he was leaning, he remained staring at the bridge and the ravine.

My grandfather used to tell me this story:

'My father was a great man, the head of his tribe and the leader of his people. When the French came banging on our doors with their mighty weapons, our tribe was well armed and our lands were impenetrable. Our people fought valiantly.

'The French sent secret emissaries to my father, promising to give him land and keep him as head of his tribe on condition that he allow them entry into the country. They even promised safe passage for himself and all the members of his family.'

My grandfather then spoke to the fighters from his tribe:

'Instead of being on the defensive, we will attack. But don't fire until I give you the signal.'

He sent word to the French, saying: 'I'll deliver the fighters to you and you give me all that you promised.'

'My father went out with his men and when they found themselves in an ambush, he instructed them not to be foolish and risk their lives. They surrendered, realizing that their past and future were in God's hands.

'My father opened the gates of the country.

'The French came into the area and killed everyone capable of bearing arms. They raped our women and made them pregnant. They decorated my father with fancy medals and proclaimed him leader of the people. They gave him lots of land. They gave him everything.'

My father used to tell this story:

'Your grandfather was a great man. He inherited from his father medals of honour, power and land. The women had their babies and the land became populated once again with men capable of bearing arms. The French decided to recruit them to fight in their wars against Morocco and Tunisia. But this time the men revolted and fled into the mountains. Your grandfather assembled an army and attacked them. Some were killed and some were saved. Others fled to the east!

'The medals kept piling up on your grandfather's chest. His titles of honour swelled as did his head. But he had to share the land with the colonialists.'

My father never achieved the grandeur of his father or his grandfather, but he was a great man in his own right. He was able to hold onto his father's land and even some of his medals. When he returned from the Syrian campaigns, they adorned him with a red burnous and elevated him to 'commander'. He was the only Algerian to possess land besides all the colonialists.

'My son,' my father used to say, 'the Boularwahs are an illustrious family, radiant in their glory and wealth. But there is one stain on the family name: we lack learning and none of our kin are scholars of law, language and other such fields of learning.

'Knowledge, accompanied by wealth and glory, is the crown of splendour. The glory of our family has reached the heavens, but we never produced a king in the real sense. So go to Tunisia and bring back the crown! Come back a king and I guarantee you a position as judge in Constantine.

'I notice that those of us who master the French sciences never achieve anything of great distinction. No matter how much they learn, they never surpass the French in any way. If, on the other hand, you were to come back with knowledge that eludes your own people, then they will submit themselves to you and even the French will be in need of your services in order to stay in power. Both you and I will have positions of influence. Your older brother will have a career in the army and you will have one at the Zaytouna Mosque.'

I got married before going to Tunisia. I was fifteen and she was only nine. The horsemen came from all over and they brought in singers and musicians. Sheep were slaughtered and magnificent feasts were arranged. They dressed me in a silk burnous and shiny leather slippers. At night, they led me in a procession to my bride.

They explained to me what I was supposed to do, but I refused to stay with her. I started to cry and so did she. Our sobbing reached such a pitch that my father heard us. He came into the room where we were and beat us both with a cane. He forced us to sleep together while the women outside our window ululated with joy.

A week later my father informed me that it was time to go. The bags were packed and we spent a night in Constantine and a night at Souk Ahras. He left me with some acquaintances of his, bade me farewell and left. When I went back home the following summer, I discovered that my wife Aisha was gone. They told me that she had died. I mourned for her even though I didn't feel as though she were my wife. I never really understood what it meant to be a husband or to be married. All I knew was that she slept beside me and that she put the covers on me and played with me and at times she cried for her mother and father.

They said she had died.

My father's youngest wife said something odd. She said that my father killed her, that he strangled her. He left his four wives one day and sent for her to come and wash his feet. He closed the door behind her and remained alone with her in the room. The next morning, we found her dead. We found blood all over her nightgown. Her neck was blue, her face was blue. There were finger marks all over her neck. We mourned for her and buried her without even washing the body. According to your father, she was too young to know what sin was.

My father's youngest wife was sixteen years old. She tried to seduce me. At first I pushed her away, but eventually I gave in.

News of my oldest brother's death came to us, but I felt no sadness whatsoever. They say that his wife died the same death as Aisha.

The years in Tunisia, stressful as they were, went by quickly. I finished my studies and went home. My father bought me a white *jubba* and a Tunisian-style fez with a black silk tassel. He took me to Constantine where we rode in a carriage drawn by a white horse. We made the customary rounds, then went to the Central Café in the main square where we sat face to face.

He used to say: 'Let's be great Algerians instead of being ordinary Frenchmen.'

My father was fiercely proud of being an Algerian, even though he was totally insensitive to other Algerians whom he regarded merely as servants and workers, like stones in a valley suited only to be trampled on.

When fighting broke out between the Muslims and the Jews, my father acted like the big hero. He attacked the neighbouring farm, which was owned by a Jewish colonial settler. He was able to take him prisoner but prevented his sharecroppers from killing him. My father had all the furniture removed from the man's house. He harnessed the farmer's horses and cattle to the threshing machines and had them moved over to his tent. He then spoke to the sharecroppers:

'You won't have much work to do, but at least you'll get one-seventh of the yield. Of course, I get four-sevenths, the owner gets two-sevenths and you will get the rest.'

No one dared to contest this decision. They all knew too well that they wouldn't starve as long as he was there.

Later that night the police came along with a group of heavily armed Jews. They blocked off the farm and demanded that my father give himself up. My father refused to surrender. He knew that his fate would be none other than death. He yelled out to the police:

'Expel the Jews and I'll surrender. My father is the Agha Boularwah and my grandfather was the Pasha Agha Boularwah who opened the gates of this country to the French. My father delivered the people to the French. I fought on their behalf in Morocco and Syria, in Aleppo, Homs and Tartus. We all received the *Légion d'honneur*.

'Expel the Jews and I'll turn myself in. I am a law-abiding citizen. This conflict is between us and the Jews, not between us and the French.'

The Jews remained alongside the police and gunfire broke out in all directions. When darkness fell over the land, my father mounted a black stallion and escaped in the night. The clans of Belbey, Ben Jaloul and Mami intervened on my father's behalf. Of course, he was forced to sell off most of his booty to pay the bribes.

My father was granted clemency in view of his past and his father's and grandfather's past. But three months later they discovered his body in Constantine. He had been thrown into the ravine from the top of the bridge, his body riddled with wounds.

Three months later, my father's youngest wife Hanifa died the same death as Aisha and my brother's wife. She used to act as though she were my wife. She waited on me hand and foot and always took my side in every household squabble. She'd act coyly with me and arrange to meet me in the house wherever it was possible.

My mother didn't say anything about it other than occasionally to bemoan the fact that she hadn't given me a sister but that God made up for it with this poor, miserable Hanifa. She used to say that this house had more hopes in it than men and that my father's other wives gave birth to children who died in the cradle. She reminded me that I was her last child. She told me once:

'Your father, may God have mercy on his soul, abandoned all four of us wives in the end and went and married a Jewish woman in Constantine. Poor Hanifa was still too young then and her patience had its limits.'

My father's second wife used to say about me:

'He's got the head of an owl, a real jinx if ever I saw one. Ever since he's come into this world, he's caused one catastrophe after another. Every newborn in this house dies. His father marries one woman after another. He saw his own wife's death, his brother's and his sister-in-law's. Now it's the father's turn. He'll bury us all. He'll be left alone, a hermit without family and neighbours. He will be the destruction of the house of Boularwah.'

My father's third wife acted the role of a mother-in-law. Whenever Hanifa became angry, she would become angry. And if Hanifa became angry at her, she would be nice to me. She used to bathe Hanifa and put fine perfumes on her. Whenever she saw me, the only thing she could talk about was Hanifa.

One night my mother knocked on my bedroom door. Hanifa jumped up in her nightgown to open the door. My mother was praying to God, praising His kindness and begging for His mercy. She told Hanifa to tell me that there was someone who had come asking about me. Hanifa came back and told me what was going on. I stared at her. My heart filled with viscous fluid. It seeped all the way up to my eyes. I had this terrible, burning sensation in my mouth and the oozing liquid inside me grew thicker.

The image of Aisha and her bruised neck flashed before my eyes, along with the finger marks on her neck. I could also see my brother's wife. Everything else went blank on me. The oozing liquid was pouring outside my body as well. I threw myself on top of her as she gasped for air. She submitted and her face turned blue. My fingers left their marks on her neck. We buried her. A week later my mother died. A week after that, my father's second wife ran away. The following week my father's third wife was laid to rest.

I left the village and made my way to Constantine, where I became involved in working with the Reformist movement.

My second wife insisted over and over again that I give her a baby. She waited patiently the first year, the second year, the third and the fourth. At the beginning of the fifth year she announced that she felt something moving in her stomach. I was delighted to hear the news. Then a week later she was gone. There was no trace of her for several years until I found out that she was living in France with her cousin, who was the real father of the baby.

I went back to the village. The wife of a sharecropper caught my eye. She was very pretty. I brought her and her daughter into my house and kept them locked in. The husband moped around for several days, then came to see me one night.

'Good evening, Shaykh.'

'Good evening to you, too.'

'I'd like to have a word with you, if I may.'

'What do you want? Don't you have enough to eat?'

'Yes, I do.'

'Do you need something?'

'No.'

'Has someone been mistreating you?'

'No.'

'Then what is it? What do you want to say?'

'I want to tell you . . . that people . . .'

'What about these people?'

'They're talking.'

'Can I stop people from talking?'

'I mean . . .'

'What do you mean? Get out of my sight, leave me alone.'

The sharecropper went away, dragging his feet. Before he reached the wall of the stable, he turned back and looked in my direction. He stood several moments, just staring. For the next several days, he hung around, moping, then finally approached me once again.

'Good evening, Shaykh.'

'Ah, it's you again! You've come back.'

'Yes, it's me.'

'Now what do you want?'

'People are talking.'

'What are they saying?'

'They're calling me a cuckold.'

'So why should that bother you?'

'The fact is, Sidi Shaykh, I'm embarrassed to talk to you about this. My grandfather worked for your grandfather and my father worked for your father. I worked for your father and now for you. Your dear departed mother was very kind to me. She was the one who arranged my marriage.'

'As far as I can see, you have two choices. You can either go and work in France or I can have you sent to Cayenne.'

'Take my daughter and return her mother to me.'

'Or you can go to France or you can disappear.'

'As you wish, Shaykh.'

The next day I put him on a ferry to Marseilles. I expected that the sharecropper's wife would get pregnant and so she did. Several months passed and one night her daughter came and knocked on our bedroom door, said something to her mother and went away. The fire was burning in the heater in our room and that viscous liquid was oozing inside me. It was even coming out of my pores, soaking my whole body. The image of Aisha flashed before me, then my sister-in-law and Hanifa. I went totally blank. I was engulfed in darkness. The next morning they found her all blue with finger marks covering her neck. We buried her that day.

I returned to Constantine with her daughter. She was Aisha's age. I recited the opening verse of the Qur'an and then I felt her stomach. Every time she complained of a belly ache, I rushed to put my hands on her stomach.

A year later, two years later, the girl grew up and came to understand my fixation with her stomach. She started to stay away from the house more and more and asked me often when I would be taking a trip. When I told her I would be going away the next day, her eyes gleamed with delight. When the next day came, I took my suitcase and left the house. I spent several hours making the rounds in the city, then went home. My sudden return surprised her. Her face turned red, then she went pale. Her lips quivered and her knees were knocking. I looked her up and down and she lowered her eyes to avoid my stare.

'What have you done?' I shouted.

'Nothing.'

'What were you intending to do?'

I put my hands on her chin and lifted her face.

'Look at me. Look me straight in the eye.'

She lifted her eyes, then lowered them quickly. I was aroused by the flush of her cheeks, her black eyes and ruby lips. I pulled at her chin and she offered no resistance. I leaned over and planted a kiss on her lips. Then I put my arms around her and pressed her body against mine.

'I want to give it to you. I know you've been waiting for one impatiently. I'm only yours. You alone. I've done nothing with anyone else.'

She kept repeating this over and over again, all the way out on the desert road, as tears welled from her beautiful eyes. A week later, I buried her and returned home.

I swore that I would never marry again. But seven months later, for reasons unbeknownst to me, I felt terrified at the thought of being alone. At night, the darkness would creep into my soul. There seemed to be a reservoir of viscous liquid that oozed inside me every time I felt the heat. It would flood my insides. I would turn on the light but see nothing. I'd reach out to touch something and feel nothing. My servants told me that in the night I would yell out: 'Aisha'. The only thing I remember is that I was filled with darkness, then my blood would come to a boil and I would drip and drown in sweat. I'd go blind, then try to reach out to touch something with my fingers.

I imagined myself marrying seven women all at once, each with her own eunuch.

I imagined myself marrying twenty women and marrying each one of them off to seven men.

I imagined buying one hundred children.

I imagined myself turning into a woman, then marrying a million men and having a million children.

I imagined digging a huge pit, as wide as the Rhumel Valley and throwing into it a thousand women, children, fathers and mothers and pouring on top of them rivers of mothers' milk.

I imagined all of that but did absolutely nothing about it. However,

I did finally end up marrying two women at the same time. I used to tell myself, one is for power, the other is for knowledge. Sometimes I used to tell myself, one is for Arabism, the other for Berberdom, or one for Islam and one for Christianity.

Whenever I looked at the two of them, I imagined a pair of opposites. I considered myself more powerful than other men. In fact, I felt like a king.

When I struck the one, I struck the other. When I kissed or slept with the one, I kissed or slept with the other. At the same time, I'd ask both of them when they were going to get pregnant. One morning I woke up and I knew that they were gone. A few days later I received a summons from the judge with two requests to dissolve the marriage contracts.

I went back to my solitude. I held land in my hands and knowledge and science in my head. I could climb the highest mountain and descend the steepest slope. But whenever I examined my situation closely, I felt myself stagnating. I was growing old and senile like the rock of Constantine, about to burst and crumble. All around me the ravine was growing damp with the flow of dirty water.

I met a Jewish woman. She said:

'I'm barren and you're impotent. So let's get married and adopt a son.'

We got married.

She waited on me hand and foot, just as she was supposed to do. She took excellent care of me and changed the way I was living for the better. We travelled to France. She was rich and more than willing to spend her money. The truth of the matter is that she was the perfect wife. I was simply overjoyed with her, or at least, I was content to the utmost.

The day we decided to adopt was the day we began to quarrel.

'Let's adopt a Jewish boy.'

'No, it must be a Muslim.'

'A Jew. After all, I'm the one who's paying for it.'

'A Muslim. I and my money are better than you and yours.'

'Then we'll adopt two: a Muslim girl and a Jewish boy.'

'No, a Muslim boy and a Jewish girl.'

'A Muslim boy and a Jewish boy.'

'I can't have a Jewish male living in my house.'

'You're a lunatic.'

'You're the lunatic.'

'No, you are.'

I slapped her and she slapped me back. Then she left the house and divorced me. I was out of my mind and she was too. I had been consumed by an arrogance that was totally uncalled for. In the end, I was the loser. I lost her money and the chance to live a good life.

I'm sorry for what I've done to you, Sara. I cry for you and the son who never came into my house, whether Jewish, Christian or Muslim. I cry from the bottom of my heart for having lost you both. We should never have quarrelled, so why did we? Our wealth and our sterility brought us together. Depravity united us. So why did we quarrel? What difference did it make what religion he was? He could have been a pagan for all it mattered. You were so stupid, but I was more so. Either way, our religion failed us both. Whatever happens, being separated or together, we are united in spirit. We'll always be husband and wife no matter how far apart we become. The desire for the son who was never born will always bind us together.

My solitude didn't last very long. I couldn't bear it. When it became increasingly difficult for me to marry a young girl and wait for her to reach puberty, my only option was to marry a deflowered woman, a widow or divorcee. I began my escape from solitude. I thought about Aisha, my wife to whom I was never really married. I thought about my sister, who was nursed on a different breast. I thought about my daughter, who was not my flesh and blood.

It was during a trip to Biskra that I met her. She had received an inheritance at Sidi Uqba. We got married and put her inheritance into other investments just as we joined together our tortured spirits. Like me, she felt this constant gloom inside her soul. She suffered seizures every new moon. First she would start to whimper, then she would burst into uncontrollable sobbing. She would dig her nails into her cheeks and tear at her clothes. She would fall to the floor and swoon in and out of consciousness for forty hours. After that she would get up and ask me what happened. At first I was greatly troubled by these fits. But after a while, I became used to them and even looked forward to them. She mourned openly for Aisha, Hanifa, Sara, my father, my brother and his wife. Her soul was full of darkness.

One night following one of her seizures she got up and left my bed. We were intimate with each other only on holidays and the only thing we ever talked about was her inheritance, especially after I got rid of her brother, Ammar. *You fight fire with fire*, as the saying goes.

'How many tons of iron do you think there are in a bridge?' asked a man standing close by.

Shaykh Boularwah turned towards him somewhat alarmed and looked him up and down.

'What's important is the technology they use, not the quantity of the material,' responded the man's companion.

Shaykh Boularwah watched them closely. They had full beards and long hair and were wearing blue jeans and T-shirts. They had similar facial features and they were both broad-shouldered and muscular, flat in the stomach and lean.

Students, he thought to himself, as he turned his glance towards the ravine and found himself muttering.

How deep is this ravine! At the bottom flows the dark, dirty water while the birds hover gloomily over it. The rock is eroding while the low-life continue to proliferate on top of it. Sooner or later, it will cave in and no longer be able to bear their weight. They will have to stand by helplessly, looking on in fear and confusion. They're living through the earthquake and they don't even know it.

These people are incapable of building bridges such as this. They can't even dig tunnels and caves. They will never be able to raise this rock. They can only press their weight down onto it.

No, Sidi Rashid, choose the first solution. Bring on a devastating fire or a great epidemic that has no cure. My great-grandfather,

grandfather, father and myself, we've all walked on this great rock. It was on this rock that the hearts of the Boularwah family beat, at times joyously, at times in great distress, sometimes in glory and sometimes in defeat. Preserve it for us, Sidi Rashid, at least as a reminder; for this rock is the Boularwah dynasty's true object of veneration.

'There will be a total breakdown in the system unless they undertake a comprehensive review. They need to consider the latest technology and adopt a revolutionary spirit that knows neither hesitation nor compromise.'

'But look, look at all of this. This is a major agricultural area, just like the rest of Algeria, like all of Africa and even Asia. Every one of the developing countries depends upon agriculture. Forty days in the summer and forty days in autumn, they work on the land. The rest of the year they sit idle.'

'They still have to do a comprehensive review, quickly, thoroughly, scientifically.'

Shaykh Boularwah couldn't help but overhear the conversation and he turned around to see where it was coming from. He guessed that the young man and woman were students since the university was close by. They were looking out over the ravine as they continued their serious conversation. He stared at them for a moment and then quite suddenly and unexpectedly shouted out loud:

'Sidi Rashid, man of miracles, bring on the fire of devastation or a killing plague! Bring us the Earthquake of Doom!'

Jisr al-Shayatin
(Demons' Bridge)

I'll leave the car at the Souk al-Asr and walk to Wool Market Square. I'll see Rizqi and then I'll take off. I won't stay in Constantine any longer than I have to.

Shaykh Abdelmajid Boularwah was thinking to himself as he drove up towards Demons' Bridge. He passed through the Jewish quarter on Belgasim Tatash Street. He drove with extra caution even though there wasn't much traffic on the road.

You never know when you'll come across kids playing in the street. The colours of the street have hardly changed at all. Ah, look, they've moved the Abdelhamid Ibn Badis Institute over to here. I wonder what they did with the old Jewish funeral parlour that used to be here? Well, what do you know: *Traditional Education and Religious Affairs.* Now that makes sense!

Jewish buildings look the same all over the world. They have the same style. They all have a plain, restrained look about them and they always have shutters on the windows. I wonder what possesses them to put up all those shutters. What are they thinking? Wherever they are, east or west, in the desert or up in the mountains, they put up shutters as though it was commanded to them in the Bible or handed down to them from one of their rabbis. Whatever the case may be, it reflects a certain spirit, a certain attitude. It's a spirit and attitude of caution and distrust on the part of the people who live inside them, jealously guarding whatever they have inside.

Whenever the windows of buildings where Jews live are boarded up, they look depressing from the outside. They give off a strong sense of being closed off from the rest of the world. They even built their state the same way they build their buildings. The shutters on the windows are firmly fastened to the walls. They look out at the world, but the world cannot look in. It isn't enough that they destroy the houses of Arabs, but they have to expel the people as well.

The Aumale High School used to be over there. Look how ugly the lettering of *Ridha Houhou* is, inscribed on the sign. Even the colour they used is so dreary it makes it look like barracks or a prison. Much of what was here now lies in ruins and the buildings are a shambles. They look as though they were here well before the French arrived and that they were built with bricks and mud instead of cement. Maybe they were here since the time of the Turks or even before that. That wicked Ibn Khaldoun used to say that the buildings of non-Arabs were stronger and more durable than those of the Arabs because the Arabs choose to build around rivers which eventually destroy them with floods and epidemics. In contrast, the non-Arabs chose to build on higher ground where the earth is firm and the air is pure. That damned Ibn Khaldoun was a writer of literature, not a historian. He was quick to see the problem but always failed to offer solutions. He could tear something apart but never put anything together. Even though he defended traditional Islam from the Mu'tazilites and the freethinking philosophers, nonetheless, he propagated his own heretical views. Ibn Khaldoun was nothing more than a one-man political movement.

In Algeria there's no beating around the bush: it's either . . . or, it's one extreme or the other, it's black or white. Take the French, for example: either they occupy Algeria by force and colonize it for a whole century or they abandon it, taking with them all those who openly supported them.

The Jews burned all their bridges when they departed. They were deceived in Algeria by people who were not of their covenant. In so doing they shut tight any window of hope. They showed their contempt for history and they allowed their intelligence to deceive them. While they preserved their identity in France, here in Algeria they gave it up in order to assume a French identity, that of the arrogant colonialist. They forgot who they were and they turned their backs on the people who were living alongside them. They were seduced by the power of the aggressor.

They used to be the masters of Constantine. They had total control over how people should act. The entire population of the east of the country obeyed them. They determined how many gold teeth a man could have in his mouth and people went along with that! They set the amount of gold a bride could have in her dowry and people accepted this decision. They specified what cloth people should wear and on what occasions. They controlled all aspects of trade, but in spite of all this, they yielded to the higher interests of colonialism. Despite the thousands of years in which they managed to maintain their identity and group solidarity, they were unable to forge their own political entity to guarantee their future.

Then suddenly they found themselves packing their bags and running away whatever way they could. Desperate, they found themselves expelled along with the French. They had dug a deep chasm between themselves and the Arabs and the bridge by which they fled was haunted by demons.

There is a theory which claims that Judaism is a spirit which is sustained by a belief in the need to engage in commerce as the only means of livelihood and that any individual or group can be converted to Judaism simply by sharing this belief. There is an element of truth in this theory. The Jews of Algeria, through their involvement in trade, came to amass great power in the country with their ability to employ, control land and engage in certain industries.

However, they were deceived. They abandoned their Jewishness and turned their backs on history. When the French departed, defeated and mortally wounded, the Jews were forced to follow them, dragging on their backs the wreckage of their Jewishness.

I wonder what would have happened had they remained. What would have become of Constantine, Algiers, Oran and Tlemcen if they still had their large Jewish populations? Would these cities still have been dominated by them commercially and economically?

Things would probably not be as bad as they are now! Most of the villagers who invaded the cities would have remained in the country-side. And the political situation would not have been so tense and radicalized. There would have been frequent and forceful interventions to keep matters from getting out of hand.

Life would not be as confusing as it is today. You would be able to go into a two- or three-star café or a tea room and not have to see young people fondling one another or see an old man reading the Qur'an or praying with his prayer beads sitting next to someone selling eggs or some kind of junk. You would not see a wealthy man forced to rub elbows with some good-for-nothing vagabond.

People used to at least respect the dividing lines that Almighty God created between them, knowing that He made people in different ranks and stations. But the nobility became a minority unable to stave off the hordes of riff-raff. They launched protests and made appeals. Ultimately they could only resist by closing themselves off from the rest of the people until they were eventually swallowed up in the tide.

Had the Jews remained in the city, Belbey would never have sunk to the depths that he has. Nor would 'the vault' have sloped as much as it has. La Brèche Square would not have deteriorated to the extent that it has, becoming a sleazy market-place where people sit around and play dominoes. The gardens would have remained a refuge for young lovers, not a hangout for tea vendors who pollute the air with their coal braziers and those other people who peddle rancid dates and rotten chickpeas.

The Jews of Algeria were not very clever. In fact, they were the least clever Jews in the world. They weren't even real Jews. It's true that the Algerians have a violent disposition which leaves no room for middle ground or moderation when solving problems. They have a backward, village mentality that leads them from one extreme to another in no time at all. If they want to die, they die all together. When they decide to live, they do so in groups, even if the foot of one is on the neck of the other and even if one lays claim to the other's land!

I think I'll turn left over here by that dilapidated building and rest for a while. The Kittaniya shrine is right near here. I wonder what's happened to it.

Shaykh Abdelmajid Boularwah veered towards the left in his car and found himself in the middle of the Souk al-Asr. He stopped in front of a building that stored gas bottles, crates of soap and barrels of cooking oil, but he wasn't sure whether they were empty or full. There were also sacks of cracked wheat. The stench of rot was overwhelming.

He turned to the right and noticed a sign on the door of a synagogue written in both French and Hebrew: *This Is My House and It Shall Be a Place of Worship for All Peoples.*

I wonder why they hung up that verse, prophetic saying, proverb or whatever it is. What is it that they're trying to say, these people who have declared themselves to be one people and one people only? They shut the doors of their synagogues in the faces of others, individuals or groups, then went right ahead and built a huge synagogue at the expense of Muslims and Christians. Why is this synagogue reserved only for them and off limits to everyone else? Indeed it would be an awkward invitation to pass through a door that has been closed to you. Perhaps they had it built in a burst of jealousy or in defence against the Catholic church that was used unabashedly to convert Algerians.

It was merely to appear tolerant and open to Europeans that they were prompted to write their verse in French alongside Hebrew. Their inferiority complex as Semites with French nationality forced them to see themselves as equal in stature to their masters. May God damn them! However, it would have been much better for us, the nobility, upper classes, landowners, merchants and businessmen, imams and judges, had they stayed!

'The winds don't always blow in favourable directions!'

These people of ours are destined to do everything to extremes and without any sense of shame. An old man reads the Qur'an while a young man sits next to him kissing his girlfriend. The majestic Panorama Hotel sits right in front of the Bardo slum. The Mosque of Sidi Rashid is a stone's throw away from the Bab al-Jabiya brothel. And here you have a synagogue sitting cheek by jowl with the Kittaniya shrine.

Shaykh Abdelmajid Boularwah locked the doors of his car and headed towards the Souk al-Asr. He noticed that the Kittaniya shrine was still painted green. He was thinking of the past.

Shaykh Ibn Badis was at war with this shrine. Now it's been turned into a vocational school. The freedom fighters ended up executing its shaykh. When its shaykh dies, so does the shrine!

They say that the commander of those freedom fighters was put in charge of the shrine but was then removed. They say he went off to Algiers and then returned. Certainly, those who restored him to his position must have figured that it was the future well-being of the shrine that was the important thing. But now it has become a national vocational school. So it wouldn't have made any difference in the world if this miserable lout had been a director, janitor or even a prison guard.

The custodian of a shrine, the director of a vocational school, a high-school principal, all these things are better than being a communist or a sieve-maker, even if my nephew Abdelqadir is one himself. Ah, there's a school next to the vocational school, Saleh Bey High School. There's the mosque. I'm glad to see it's still a mosque and that at least some of our traditions have survived. I'd bet everything I have that the custodian sticks his hands in the cookie jar and makes off with people's offerings.

Why does this insufferable crowd, the countless number of men, women and children floating in a sea of rotting fruit and vegetables, persist in following me everywhere I go? It seems as if every one of the half-million people who live in this city heard my footsteps and came out on the street to keep me from finding my relatives, with no other purpose than to prevent me from carrying out my grand scheme.

The darkness is returning to my soul. My temperature's rising and the viscous fluid is oozing inside me.

This city is one huge ruin. It looks like the dregs of a market-place on a main boulevard. It's in shambles like Bardo, Sidi M'sid and the Boulfarayis dump. If God hadn't blinded its inhabitants in order to hasten their destruction, they would have taken all the earth with which they built their hovels and thrown it into the bottom of the ravine. They would have had the insight to lift the weight that they impose on this rock. Had they not been blinded, they would have awaited their impending doom in tents and refugee shelters. Since they don't know right from wrong, what difference would it have made if they lived in one huge tent where they could sleep on top of one another and commit their abominations, where they could buy and sell, eat and steal, tear their shoes apart and sew them back together again?

In fact, they wouldn't even have to wear any shoes at all, since whatever they accomplish, they do it sitting on their butts. Let their godless government set up for them four or five such refugee camps so that they understand what socialism and communism are really all about. Let them see what they're getting into. Clue them in on what's in store for them once the new policies are put into effect.

Look all around, here you see the old cobblers, the pigeons, thousands of prickly pear rinds and smells that overwhelm you wherever you are. Even the walls in this place are caving in.

When Sidi Rashid gives the signal, when the momentous event takes place, when every suckling female forgets her suckling and pregnant women abort their foetuses, demons will be dispatched in every direction. All the bridges that sit on top of the ravine will discharge their load into it and, of course, the part of the ravine that sits below Demons' Bridge will receive the lion's share. The slope will become steeper and the crowds will multiply. The darkness will increase in my heart and the oozing liquid will creep throughout my body.

I wonder what ever happened to Rizqi, the saddler, my father's cousin. The last time I saw him he was about forty years old. He wasn't able to contribute in any way to the war effort and I doubt if he had any prospects. What could a saddle-maker possibly do, with the number of donkeys and mules dwindling these days? Besides, with all the saddle-makers you find, it's a wonder that he could even have such a profession. Rizqi could never be an officer or a martyr, professor or teacher. He could never be a minister or an advisor or a local government official. If things changed and it happened that he was no longer able to make a living making saddles, then he could easily have become a cobbler or a tailor. Perhaps if he got lucky and things turned out for the better, he may have become an electrician or a plumber with a couple of apprentices to help him out. Be that as it may, what's important to bear in mind is that a saddler doesn't become a government employee nor could he ever join the government in any shape or fashion.

Where am I? Why haven't I reached Wool Market Square? It's not that far away from the Souk al-Asr. The man riding that donkey over there looks like he may have bought that saddle from Rizqi. God damn him! Look at him, he's barefoot and wearing a necktie. He's got a cigarette in his mouth and he's wearing a European wool hat on his half-shaven head. The man on the beast in reverse!

Where am I? The odours are pungent and it's getting dark. There seem to be more and more people on the streets. I must be close to a market. That old man over there looks so stupid with his head bowed, sitting among the feet of pedestrians with a basket of henna and a pile of children's school bags. All these cars are trying to part the human waves. I'm lost!

Shaykh Boularwah stopped and tried to get his bearings. What caught his eye was the writing on a sign for a private school. Facing it was a sign in a shop window that read: *The Elegance of Young Muslim Girls*. Brassieres, girdles, women's undergarments. May God damn this merchant in the light of day and the dark of night.

The call to prayer came over the loudspeaker. It was excessively loud and he wondered why it was so.

'They've got the record on the wrong speed,' sneered a young man as he passed by.

God damn him, damn them all, Sidi Rashid. O Lord, bring on the chaos, the earthquake, the plague. Spare not one of them, but grant me pardon and all of my family.

'A nice plump turkey, uncle?'

'How about some cracked wheat for Ramadan?'

'Hey, uncle, how about a can of Danish cheese?'

'Some good-luck charms: *The Impenetrable Fortress* or *The Perfumed Garden*?'

'Interested in an eighteen-carat gold chain?'

'Hey, my little gazelle, how about coming for a ride with me in my car?'

'Drop dead, low-life!'

'What's wrong with you? None of the eggs broke.'

'Fancy speech has lost its taste. Clever words now lie in waste.'

The sound was blasting from a music shop with words that had a distinctive Moroccan accent. Everything was becoming utterly confusing to Shaykh Abdelmajid Boularwah.

If I ask for directions, they'll know that I'm a stranger in town and they'll follow me like a pack of wolves. They're all bandits and thieves. I'd better ask one of the merchants. Lord help me, where have all the real merchants gone? These peddlers aren't merchants at all. They've abandoned their flocks and thrown away their rods, they've assaulted our cities and taken over our businesses and homes. They marry our daughters and take on whatever social rank or profession they desire.

I'll ask this old man coming up my way. He's clearly a city man who's suffering from what's ailing this city. The feeling of the imminent Earthquake of Doom must be getting to him. Here he comes!

An old woman shoved him as she passed by and he moved quickly to get out of her way. A young man stepped on his foot and a man selling chickens blocked his way. He stopped walking. As he turned, a car was passing and prevented him crossing the street. A small child squeezed between his legs to pass through. He moved aside in an attempt to avoid all of them. He resolved to walk through the thick of the crowd with all the deftness of a tourist guide.

'In which direction is Wool Market Square, may God keep you and yours, my good man?'

Hardly had he finished his question than the old man disappeared. Having been tripped up by a teenager and swallowed up in a crowd of old women, he was nowhere in sight.

I'll throw myself into the wave of people and push myself along with it until I find a way out of this no man's land. Should I go down or up? They seem to be going in all different directions, up and down. I feel like we're at the bottom of a river or at the bottom of the ocean that is being pressured from all sides, being jerked back and forth, up and down, taking along with it mud, sand, pebbles, seaweed and dead fish. I feel like we're in the midst of a whirlpool that keeps spinning around.

The same old streets, the same odours and goods, the same faces in every corner of the city. If you head upwards, you get lost, if you go downwards, you still get lost. No sooner do you come across something that appears vaguely familiar than it vanishes altogether. The only things that are left of Constantine are its mosques, shrines, mausoleums, bathhouses and stalls that roast sheep's brains. But all these things no longer have what they used to have. They announce the call to prayer from the mosques with electric loudspeakers or with poor-quality recordings. The shrines are now vocational schools and high schools. The bathhouses are public toilets and God knows whose brains they're roasting in these stalls. For all I know, it's probably dogs and wolves.

I think I'll go down the hill. Wool Market Square is further away than the Souk al-Asr. I'll throw myself into the crowd that's headed in that direction and let it lead me to the end. There has to be a main street at that point from where I can either get back to my car or find Wool Market Square.

Shaykh Abdelmajid Boularwah threw himself onto the street and into the wave of pedestrians. An ocean of hands and shoulders was tossing him about and feet on all sides were trampling on his toes. Cars were beeping at him and the vendors on the streets blocked his way every few feet.

I am in the Sinai Desert.

I'm in the middle of nowhere.

I'm in the Jewish quarter. Where are you, Sara? Do I find you in the East or West? What did you do about all those things you and I dreamed of?

What can I do about all this obnoxious noise droning in my ears? There must be a hundred trucks passing through here every hour on their way to Annaba and Skikda. The entire city has become one big industrial zone. Just imagine, the street is collapsing more and more each day. From all the weight it has to bear it's barely passable.

'On the contrary, the government has made great strides in the area of industrialization.'

'In education, too. Ever since the townships became responsible for building schools there isn't one single hamlet in Algeria left without a school. Even those that have to wait a year or more for a teacher are building schools and knocking on all the right doors.'

'France never left behind a national infrastructure for building a nation.'

'They could have done something so that at least some of us would be living in the twentieth century.'

'Thief, thief! Grab that thief!'

'When an earthquake struck Constantine in 1947, everyone thought that was the end for the city.'

'I was a kid then and the only thing I remember were waves of people running away, screaming for help in different languages.'

'I was about twenty, so I can still see it as though it was right in front of me. Hundreds and hundreds of children's bodies were lying on the street. Some of them had been so stamped upon by the fleeing mobs that they looked like slabs of meat. Some of them were still moving and others weren't injured at all. There were people running in great panic. I can still hear the pounding footsteps and the screams of women and children.'

'They say that there was carbide at the heart of the rock.'

'Others say it was salt.'

'They released all the progressives they arrested.'

'That's just a first step. I don't understand how they could call this a socialist country when all the socialists are in jail.'

'You're right. There is still one distinction which our country merits, and if it remains intact, then it will be a lesson for future generations: there has been no turning to bloodshed. Of all the events that have taken place since independence, there has not been one incident of execution of political prisoners. Can you imagine? No matter how heinous the crime or bitter the conflict, this country has not witnessed one political execution or assassination.'

'I agree. But do you think that if reactionaries come to power or come close to it, they won't resort to bloodshed? Hardly! Class struggle is inevitable and there isn't a class that would rule without violence and bloodshed.'

'Hey, uncle, want to buy some goose eggs? You can even let 'em hatch!'

'He brought the car back from France practically new. It wasn't more than four years old. He thought he'd use it for a while until he could sell it or find a job. He decided to use it as an unlicensed taxi. The police found out and gave him a choice: either sell it to them dirt cheap or they would confiscate it. He promised to sell it to them. Then he decided to bring it back to France, but they were one step ahead of him. Do you know what happened?'

'No.'

'He poured gasoline all over it and set it on fire.'

'He's crazy.'

'There will soon be a debate on the proposals for agricultural reform.'

'Is that so?'

'Yes, very soon, in fact. I heard about it at the last meeting in Algiers. This year they hope to put it into effect.'

'That would be a great event, like the start of the revolution or getting our independence. But the fact of the matter is that it's coming too late. Nine years after gaining our independence and nothing in this area has happened. Look at all these people! They're all running away from the countryside where all you find is unemployment, hunger, disease and ignorance. As God is my witness, in Collo, Aures, Souk Ahras and Tebessa, they still live in the Middle Ages.'

The heat became more intense. Shaykh Abdelmajid Boularwah could feel the viscous fluid frothing at his mouth and pouring out of his eyes and nose. It was oozing all over his body and that gloomy darkness made everything look invisible. He no longer knew where he was. He thought about whether or not to talk to someone. Would he be pushed backwards or forwards or would he be twirled around in one place?

'Where is my brother-in-law Ammar, the barber?'

'Ammar the barber died a martyr.'

'Where is my cousin Abdelqadir, the sieve-maker?'

'Abdelqadir Boularwah is a professor.'

'Where is Tahir Boularwah, the pickpocket?'

'Tahir Boularwah, the pickpocket, is a high-ranking officer with power and influence.'

'Where is my nephew, Issa Boularwah, the custodian at the shrine?'

'Issa Boularwah, the custodian at the shrine, is a communist who leads an underground life.'

'And what about my father's cousin Rizqi, the saddler?'

'Rizqi, the saddler, is an imam in a mosque.'

'Praise be to God.'

'No, a government minister.'

'Praise be to God.'

'No, a martyr. No, a traitor. No, an imam. Minister, president.'

'May God be praised on high!'

He was drowning in a wave of people as he spoke out loud.

Children followed him and laughed raucously at him, repeating every word he said.

'Where am I, where am I?' he screamed as loud as he could.

The children answered back all at once:

'At Demons' Bridge, Demons' Bridge.'

He opened his eyes. In front of him was the Joan of Arc High School. Her wings were open and she was ready to fly. He saw the hospital, the granary and the train station. A whistle was blowing. He felt awful and he turned around. This used to be the Jewish quarter.

'I'm at Demons' Bridge for sure.'

He shuddered with fear. The viscous fluid and that dark gloom overpowered him. He began to run up the hill shouting out loud:

'O people of Constantine. The Earthquake of Doom, the Earthquake of Doom is coming. Beware, Boularwah family. The earthquake has come!'

Jisr al-Hawa'
(Bridge of the Abyss)

Shaykh Boularwah decided to run the distance that separated Demons' Bridge from the Bridge of the Abyss. When he arrived, he was sweating profusely. He turned in the direction of Sidi M'sid and took a long, deep breath. He then looked towards the Qantara Bridge and took another deep breath.

It's no use. The air is stifling and the humidity is unbearable. There's no end to it in sight.

A car passed by and the bridge started to shake back and forth. It shook with sporadic convulsions. His heart was pounding and his chest was throbbing. The shouts of the children were piercing his ears:

'Boularwah, Boularwah.'

He opened his eyes and stared intensely at the children. They had formed a long line behind him. A man scolded them and they ran away. They stopped at the front of the bridge and continued shouting:

'O Ammar, Abdelqadir, Tahir, Issa, O Rizqi, O Boularwah.'

'Am I dreaming or am I awake?'

He kept an eye on them as they congregated around the entrance to the bridge.

There they are, sons of Aisha, of Sara, Hanifa, the sharecropper's wife, her daughter's sons. The sons of a million women and ten million men.

There's the man on the beast riding the beast. The tail of the beast will be in the east and its head in the west. A part of its belly will cover Constantine.

He bent down and stretched out his arms to grab some of the children.

'Take them, man on the beast. Take these sons of bitches and whores.'

He opened his eyes. The bridge was shaking and the jaws of the ravine were wide open.

The cries of those from above and those from below will not be heard. Not once have I ever been down below and been able to see what the top looks like from there. From the top of the bridge, the bottom looks completely flat because of the distance. The people look so small and everything looks so minuscule. The same thing happens when you look at the past. In fact, it happens whenever you look at the masses, at all these riff-raff.

There is a very narrow pass for pedestrians that has been carved out of the layers of rock. Up above is a trodden path which extends all the way to the Sidi M'sid Bridge. Beyond that is the road to Skikda which snakes along the cliff through the tunnels and passageways.

'O Aisha, my wife whom I never married, O sister, whom my father never fathered and my mother never delivered, O daughter, who was never conceived from my loins, why did your necks turn blue and reveal the traces of my father's fingerprints?'

The liquid oozed out of his eyes, nose and mouth. The dark gloom enveloped him while he heard knocking all around him. He bent down and took her neck between his hands, squeezing tighter and tighter. She drew her last breath. Instead of leaving her as she was, he picked her up by the neck and held her up in the air. He stretched out his arms and dangled her in mid-air. Then he dropped her, feet first. She fell to the bottom while her body tumbled around in her white dress. Just before she hit rock bottom, she appeared to him in a flash. She was whispering:

'Your fingers are like your father's and your hands are like his as well.'

He opened his eyes. The bridge was shaking and the children were shouting all around him:

'Bou-lar-wah.'

'They're all union members. No, students. No, riff-raff from the

Boulfarayis dump. They want to throw me into the bottom of the ravine, to the bottom of the earth. But I'll beat them to it and throw them in first.'

He bent down and tried to grab onto as many of them as he could. He wanted to throttle them before tossing them over the bridge. But he felt too weak for that, so he thought about throwing them over alive. He stretched out his arms and opened his hands. He let them go, but they didn't fall. They stayed right where they were, up on the bridge, right under his nose, looking him straight in the eye. They taunted him:

'We're from Sidi M'sid.'

'We're from the Boulfarayis dump.'

'We're from Souiqa.'

'We're from the Souk al-Asr, from Bardo, from Janan Tashina.'

'We're the children of the martyrs of Collo, Milia, Mila, the Aures Mountains, from Jurjura.'

'We're the children of the Machat workers and the labourers at the railroad. We're the children of all those who work at the Prince Abdelqadir Mosque.'

'God damn all of you. Go to hell.'

They didn't leave. They stayed and taunted him all the more.

He opened his eyes, but they were no longer right in front of him. Some were at one end of the bridge, while some were at the other. He turned in both directions quickly. He imagined them charging towards him all at once. He imagined that they were going to pick him up and throw him over the bridge and into the bottom of the ravine. He thought of shouting for help:

'O Sidi Rashid, O good people of Constantine.'

Instead he opened his eyes. The water was dark as it flowed through the ravine.

Between me and the abyss there are a million miles. Twenty million. If I fall over, I won't die. I won't reach that far. I won't let them throw me in. I'll throw myself over if I have to. No way will they throw me in.

I'm stronger than they.

I'm the brother-in-law of Ammar the barber and the uncle of Tahir the pickpocket. Abdelqadir the sieve-maker is my cousin and Rizqi the saddler is a relative of mine. I am Boularwah and son of Boularwah. The blood of Boularwah runs through my veins.

The bridge shakes as a car passes by. The tapping of a mule's hooves echoes loudly. A fire is raging inside him. The thick, hot, viscous liquid is gushing violently all through his body. The darkness all around him is blacking out the world. He imagines hearing his own voice:

'Hanifa, you, my father's wife and my wife, you were Aisha. You resembled her in every way. Why did my fingers leave their prints on your throat, just my father's left theirs on Aisha's?'

The tapping of the mule's hooves came closer. His eyes were closed and his arms were outstretched as his fingers curled inward. He grabbed hold of Hanifa's neck. He began to squeeze, harder and harder, until she drew her last breath. He carried her to the top and stretched out his arms. His fingers opened and Hanifa began to tumble down in her flimsy nightgown. Before she gave herself up to the abyss, she looked up at him and whispered:

'You're no better than your father.'

He opened his eyes. The bridge was shaking and the humidity was scorching. Both ends of the bridge were crowded with people.

They're surrounding me.

They're surrounding me from all sides, from Sidi M'sid and the Boulfarayis dump, from Souiqa and the Souk al-Asr, Bardo and Janan Tashina. The martyrs' children are surrounding me and so are the children of the Machat workers, the railroad workers and those from the Prince Abdelqadir Mosque. But I mustn't be afraid of them. I'm stronger than all of them put together. I'll take them all in one hand and throw them over the bridge and into the ravine. I made a promise to Sidi Rashid, and Sidi Rashid never disappoints those who make a promise. They'll never take away my land. I am a pious servant of God. It is He who gave me my land and elevated me to my rank.

'Bou-lar-wah, Bou-lar-wah.'

The shouting was coming from both ends of the bridge. He turned first to the left and then to the right.

They're armed! Tahir Boularwah is with them and so is Abdelqadir Boularwah. There are Ammar and Issa holding up their banners. Rizqi, the saddler, is their imam. They're going to attack, they're advancing.

'O Sidi Rashid, O good people of Constantine!'

'O Boularwah!' answered the children.

He opened his eyes.

How deep is this ravine! It has swallowed up Abraham, the friend of God, the tribes of Ad, Thamud, Jurham and Qahtan. It has devoured Tacfarinas, Jurgurtha, Nero, Uqba Ibn Nafi and Musailama.

How deep is this ravine! In its belly lie the hungry, the sons of Souiqa, Sidi M'sid, Awinat al-Foul and the Boulfarayis dump, the children of every wretched working man.

'But I'll never go down and be one of them.'

He could feel the steel cables that supported the bridge.

If only the French hadn't left, if only they would come back one way or another. If only the Jews of Algeria hadn't committed such a folly as to turn their backs on their own history. If only Belbey had found people to support him.

The volcano within him was starting to erupt. The bridge shook and the lava oozed out of his mouth, nose and eyes. Darkness enveloped him.

At the beginning of the fifth month, she announced that she felt something moving in her stomach. I was delighted to hear the news. Then a week later she was gone. There was no trace of her for several years until I found out that she was living in France with her cousin, who was the real father of the baby.

'Where are you running away to, my dear second wife? You belong here, right at my feet.'

He bent down. He put his fingers around her neck and started to squeeze with all his might. But she didn't stop breathing and her chest heaved up and down.

'I won't die. It's yourself you're strangling, not me. You're impotent. You're sterile.'

He picked her up and tossed her over the bridge. She glided towards the bottom of the ravine, but it seemed to be taking longer than usual. Just before she hit the bottom, she whispered:

'My son will return from France and throw you into the bottomless pit.'

His eyes opened.

You can hear a roaring sound whenever you're on top of the Bridge of the Abyss. If you listen very closely, you can imagine yourself hearing all of Constantine and everything that is going on in it. Whenever somebody is on the bridge, billions of waves rush towards it. Each wave carries with it the voice of a woman or a child, an old man or an animal, or a sputtering motor. The truth is that all of these voices can hardly be distinguished from one another. Even though these waves are separate from one another and flow in parallel lines, they still seem to overlap each other.

What's different on the Bridge of the Abyss is that these roaring sounds have a huge effect on your heart. That's because what the city is telling you from here has greater significance.

He felt a boiling sensation in his chest and the lava was flooding his insides. The dark gloom was blacking out everything around him.

'People are talking.'

'What are they saying?'

'They're calling me a cuckold.'

'So why should that bother you?'

'The fact is, Sidi Shaykh, I'm embarrassed to talk to you about this. My grandfather worked for your grandfather, and my father worked for your father. I worked for your father and now for you. Your dear departed mother was very kind to me. She was the one who arranged my marriage.'

'As far as I can see, you have two choices. You can either go and work in France or I can have you sent to Cayenne.'

'Take my daughter and return her mother to me.'

'Or you can go to France or you can disappear.'

'As you wish, Shaykh.'

He bent down and started to squeeze tightly with all his fingers. The sharecropper's wife drew her last breath, and after her, the daughter drew her last breath. The sharecropper was moping around his house. He wanted to tell him something. He looked at him, embarrassed. He disappeared. His wife and daughter were strangled. He threw them into the bottom of the ravine. He waited for them to hit the ground but nothing happened. They continued falling. The farther they got, the closer they seemed to him. Voices were rising. He didn't know if they were theirs or somebody else's.

'The sharecropper didn't die. He's not sterile either. One way or another he's going to come back. Now he has come back to seize your land and fill it with his children.'

'No, no!' he screamed.

Shaykh Boularwah opened his eyes. People avoided looking at him as they passed by. Only the children watched as they stood around him, taunting him with their screams.

'O Bou-lar-wah.'

The bridge is shaking. The humidity is insufferable. The sun is starting to set. A single stone slips out from underneath the rest of the rocks. Vapours are rising up from the bottom of the ravine. The heart of Constantine is full of carbide, coal and salt. The rest of the rocks start to crumble. Dust is filling the air. The bridge rises and moves further away.

The earthquake is coming.

Ah, Sidi Rashid.

People are running. Some are tumbling along with the rocks. Children's bodies are turning into slabs of meat. Gas tanks explode. The silos are crumbling. There's gas leaking everywhere and fires are breaking out. Huge flames shoot high in the sky. The bridge is getting further away. You can hear the screams everywhere. You can smell the sizzling flesh of men and animals. Every part of the city is in flames. The ravine is filling up. Sidi M'sid cannot be seen; it's disappeared. Bardo is collapsing. The Boulfarayis dump has spilled beyond its borders. The earth is sinking and Constantine is melting away. Constantine is no longer.

Only Sidi Rashid Bridge remains, supporting noble and honourable people. The Bridge of the Abyss is taking me with it, all the way down.

Yes, Sidi Rashid, you deserve a whole case of candles.

He opened his eyes. Everything is as it was.

How deep is the ravine!

Both ends of the bridge are surrounded by children. They continue calling out:

'Bou-lar-wah, Bou-lar-wah!'

Has the earthquake actually started or not? Why am I at my wit's end, anxiously anticipating impending doom? Only the real earthquake has that effect. Sidi Rashid must have heard my prayer and accepted my offering.

There's no wind, not even a breeze. The temperature is rising, the liquid is overflowing and darkness is spreading out over the horizon.

He came in dressed as a groom. He was reeking with perfume. According to his wishes, the two of them were waiting for him on the bed. He ordered them to get down from the bed. They obeyed.

You, take off my right shoe, and you, my left.

He spoke to them roughly. They obeyed. When they finished what he told them to do, he kicked both of them.

I am Shaykh Boularwah. This is my fifth marriage. I am your lord and master. What I permit you to do is permissible, what I forbid is forbidden!

They obeyed.

The two of you share one and the same desire, and I am that absolute desire. Go to sleep.

They obeyed.

I am Boularwah. You are opposites bound together by my will. You are wealth and you are knowledge. You are sacred tradition and you are reckless innovation. You are the disciple of Ibn Badis and you are a devotee of Kittaniya.

The two wives escaped while he was asleep. They went down into the gorges. They're waving their hands.

'Your will, Boularwah, has no effect on your sterility. You're impotent. Your will shall never allow you to fulfil your dream and extend your life. You're sterile.'

Even at the bottom of the ravine, they remained as two brides, sitting up on one bed, exchanging the same glance and thinking the same thought.

One opposite doesn't negate the other but in fact creates a third which looks for its own opposite.

'Bou-lar-ah, Bou-lar-wah!'

He opened his eyes.

Now all the children of the city were congregating around both ends of the bridge. Ibn Badis was with them. They covet my land. They want to steal it from me. No, never! Go to Europe. Leave this city. Go to Annaba, Skikda, Oran. There are huge factories there. There's land all laid out before your eyes. Emigrate! There's going to be a great earthquake here. Sidi Rashid himself is going to shake up the earth. I've already made an agreement with him. Go, get out of here. I'll never give up my land. I'm going to sign it over to Ammar, Tahir, Abdelqadir and Rizqi. Of course, on condition that they sell it only to another Boularwah.

The heat, the suffocation, the lava erupting from the volcano within. Is that tapping on the bridge or at the door? Who's there? Who is it?

Sara!

You'll never die because you're barren. The day you die is the day you'll disappear, body and soul. You'll be buried along with desire, passion and darkness.

Let's kill him before we adopt him, Muslim, Jew or Christian.

Strangle first his soul and I will strangle the rest. Don't commit the same sin that your people committed. The house is the house of God and He wants it to be a place of worship for all peoples. Open up the windows and don't stand behind them. Everything belongs to God, and God gives everything to His pious servants.

Go back, Sara, go back.

You're neither at the bottom of the ravine nor on top of the bridge. You're beyond the reach of the earthquake, Sara, because you and your people made a grave error. You turned your backs on history. You left Algeria and abandoned its nobility and you will continue to leave and abandon every place you go. You will die the day desire dies within you and you will know the earthquake when desire in you is reborn.

You're condemned, Sara, you and your people, along with colonialism and the nobility of this country.

'O Boularwah!'

'They're getting closer.'

They were indeed coming closer. The Bridge of the Abyss was packed at both ends. There were children and grown-ups. Some were dressed in military uniforms, others in civilian clothes.

Shaykh Ibn Badis is with them and there's both Issa and Tahir Boularwah as well. They're advancing, getting closer and closer. The chanting is getting louder:

'Fancy speech has lost its taste. Clever words now lie in waste.'

The fire is burning and the viscous liquid is oozing out of him. Darkness prevails.

You, daughter of Uqba Ibn Nafi, coming from Biskra, exchange trances with me, yours against mine. Cry for me before I jump off this bridge. Mourn for all of us Boularwahs.

Here I am, throwing my jacket, shirt, shoes and trousers over the bridge. They'll reach the bottom before I do.

'O Sidi Rashid, O good people of Constantine.'

'Bou-lar-wah!'

The children were now screaming as the police seized him just in time to stop him from killing himself. All the way to the hospital, there were three voices humming in his ear.

First there was the voice of the elderly townsman wearing a fez, yelling:

'Sidi Rashid, man of miracles!'

Next there was the sound of singing, accompanied by the *rebab*:

'Sidi Talib, cure me of what ails me.'

Finally, there was the voice with the distinctive Moroccan accent:

'Fancy speech has lost its taste. Clever words now lie in waste.'

Glossary of Names and Terms

burnous	heavy, sleeveless, wool cape-like overcoat with a hood
Ibn Badis	Algerian reformer from Constantine, leader of the Salafiyya movement in 1930s Algeria and co-founder of the Association of the Ulema, 1931
Ibn Khaldoun	Arab historian and social scientist (1332–1406)
imam	prayer leader in a mosque
jubba	traditional white linen robe worn by North African men
Kaaba	place of veneration at the Grand Mosque in Mecca
kufiyya	Arab headdress
meloukhia	Jew's mallow, a leafy spinach-like vegetable; okra in Maghribi Arabic
mihrab	prayer niche in a mosque indicating direction of Mecca
rebab	spike-fiddle used in traditional Arabic music
Shawiya	mountainous region, predominantly Berber, in north-east Algeria
shaykh	title of respect given usually to a religious scholar or an elder of a community
Sidi (Si)	(al-Sayyid) title of respect, like Mr or Sir; also used for saints
souk	traditional Middle Eastern market-place
Zaytouna Mosque	venerated mosque in Tunis considered to be one of Islam's holiest places, built in the eighth century

Bibliography

Plays
'Ala al-daffa al-ukhra (n. d.)
Al-Harib (1969)

Short Stories
Dukhan min qalbi (1965)
Al-Ta'nat (1969, 1981)
Al-Shuhada' ya'udun hadha al-usbu' (1978)

Novels
Al-Laz (1974)
Rumana (1981)
Al-Zilzal (1974)
Al-Hawwat wa al-Qasr (1980)
'Urs baghl (1978)
Al-'Ishq wa al-mawt fi al-zaman al-harashi (1980)
Tajriba fi al-'ishq (1989)
Al-sham'a wa al-dahaliz (1996)
Al-Wali al-Tahir ya'ud ila maqamih al-zaki (1999)

MIDDLE EASTERN FICTION SERIES

Agop Hacikyan & Jean-Yves Soucy

A Summer Without Dawn

560 pp; Hb 0 86356 538 7

Ghazi Algosaibi

Seven

242 pp; Hb 0 86356 088 1

Mohamed Choukri

For Bread Alone

170 pp; Pb 0 86356 138 1

Streetwise

164 pp; Pb 0 86356 045 8

Mai Ghoussoub

Leaving Beirut

188 pp; Pb 0 86356 090 3

Tawfik al-Hakim

Maze of Justice

136 pp; Pb 0 86356 200 0

Amos Kenan

The Road to Ein Harod

116 pp; Pb 0 86356 002 4

Sahar Khalifeh

Wild Thorns

208 pp; Pb 0 86356 003 2

Nawal El-Saadawi

Love in the Kingdom of Oil

190 pp; Pb 0 86356 070 9;
Hb 0 86356 079 2

The Fall of the Imam

192 pp; Pb 0 86356 069 5

Memoirs of a Woman Doctor

102 pp; Pb 0 86356 076 8;
Hb 0 86356 184 5

Two Women in One

124 pp; Pb 0 86356 026 1

Abdel Rahman al-Sharqawi

Egyptian Earth

252 pp; Pb 0 86356 261 2;
Hb 0 86356 326 0

May Telmissany

Dunyazad

120 pp; Pb 0 86356 340 6;
Hb 0 86356 552 2

Abdullah al-Udhari

Until I Was Eight

160 pp; Pb 0 86356 068 7

Tahir Wattar

The Earthquake

184 pp; Pb 0 86356 339 2;
Hb 0 86356 944 7